2

Other Books by Patrick W. Marsh

The Greenland Diaries: Days 1 – 100

The Greenland Diaries: Days 101 – 140

The Greenland Diaries: Days 141 – 200

The Greenland Diaries: Days 201 – 260

The Greenland Diaries: Days 261 – 290

The Drum: A Collection of Stories from the Greenland Diaries

The Eye in the Lace: A Collection of Stories from the Greenland Diaries

Beware the Ills

Monsters, Monsters, Everywhere

Moya

I Sing Constellations

Seven Monsters

ISBN: 9798880391035
Edition: 1st Blood, Bone, and Rust.
Copyright Patrick W. Marsh
All Right's Reserved
Minneapolis, MN

Leave the Name

And Other Stories

Cover Art by M. Cooper
By Patrick W. Marsh

This book is dedicated to my dear friends Kyle and Lainie.

Thank you for always being there for me since the beginning of this long and hard journey.

Table of Contents

The Greenland Diaries

Beware the Ills

Hidden Oaks

Factory 9

Monsters, Monsters,
Everywhere.

These are some jewels and bones to my unfinished tales. Beware the Ills, Factory 9, and so many others are living and breathing in this collection of monsters and cursed islands. These are fragments of nightmares, body parts of the beast, and crumbled bits of mortar from the haunted castle walls. I'm happy to share these ruins with you. They might be complete someday, but I can't promise anything. Enjoy the windows into these worlds while they're open.

The purpose of this collection is to give you, my loyal readers who have been wandering with me since the beginning, a bit more perspective on the worlds I first created in my self-publishing journey.

You'll meet Erasmus, a special character in the Greenland Diaries who is directly connected to the Unnamed. He is a lead plot point for the ending of the story, and the sequels in the future. From Beware the Ills, you'll meet the Three-Clawed Man, an assassin who can challenge the freshly appointed Guardian. You'll learn oodles about the Cursed Island. You'll read stories from Hidden Oaks about a monster that lives in a small park in 90's suburban Minnesota. That one is based on my teenage years in my own backyard. Beyond that, you'll have stories about Factory 9, and a bonus short story never seen before, which is specific to this collection.

I will also explain my reasoning and give valuable insights about each story at the end of the book. These are my monsters. Nobody knows them better than me.

I promise to finish these stories someday. I do have some new books on the horizon, but I won't forget about any of these worlds and their various monsters. I cannot wait to finish the Greenland Diaries and give all of you some answers about what has been happening. The Cursed Island is ripe for exploration. Factory 9 has many more rooms. Hidden Oaks is undeniably epic in scope.

These worlds are thick with undiscovered narratives.

Thank you all for your continued support. Whether you've bought my books, reviewed them, talked to me online or at conventions, all of it is appreciated. Every contribution you've made to me on this voyage of mine is beyond valuable.

As I've wrestled with mental health and personal issues, writing has been a consistent form of stability for me. It will always be there. However, without all of you reading it, my monsters would just be citizens in the graveyard of my desktop. I truly can't put into words how much you all mean to me. Thank you again.

Enjoy.

The Greenland Diaries

Erasmus

When he woke there was a cascade of reality.

His mind was lost at first. A gale of sensations throttling every sensor receptor on his body. The stench of gravel. The glare of the sun blasting through his sweaty eyelids. The casual roar of overburdened trees. They all came rushing in at once.

Eventually the sights, sounds, and feelings begin to slow down, almost taking turns, as if they knew of his confusion and unnatural state. Maybe they pitied him.

He sat up slowly. His limbs were weak, wobbly, and uncertain of what his brain wanted to do with them. He was in the center of a large pit, with yellow earth in all directions. The sediment was high enough so he couldn't see far around him. Atop the lips of dirt were the branches of trees. Their bulky, paper-shadows swayed back and forth. Ships moored lazily in the afternoon tide.

He twisted his body slightly. At his feet was a beige blanket with streaks of dried red and pink fluid. There was something ominous about those crimson patterns, but he couldn't get his mind to tell him what or why. Beneath his head was a pillow, which was also stained with dirt. He took a deep breath, propping himself up with his right hand.

"Am, am I in a quarry?" He said to himself, in a hoarse and timid voice.

How did he know that word? How did he know that language? He had no idea who he was, but he was able to speak and verbalize? How?

He slowly stood, placing his hands on his thighs for extra balance. His body was short and wiry. His hair was black, his skin tan, and he wore a red flannel shirt with khaki shorts. On his feet were a pair of tennis shoes. One was white. One was navy blue. Each was torn and ragged. The fabric was pulsing outwards in tangled threads. Something had shredded them.

Had he been walking? It looked like he had. Why was he sleeping in the middle of an empty pit?

"Hey, hey, you there?" A voice said from above. He craned his neck and stuck a shaky hand in front of his eyes to block out the sun. To his left, up high above the hole, a man was crouched over the pit. He was wearing some sort of body armor and was wrapped in a beige, partially torn plastic sheet. His skin was white, but grimy with mud. He was missing an ear, had a small face with sunken eye sockets, and a long, gray beard. He had on a black baseball cap, which had a tattered rim. He was carrying some sort of gun. The skin and tendons of his fingers were tight along the heavy metal.

"What on earth are you doing taking a nap out in the open? I mean honestly, do you want to die?" His eyes darted right and left, studying his surroundings.

Wh-what?" He stammered back.

"I said you're out in the open. Get out of there right now. Do you want to die? They'll be here any minute. The Drum is about to start."

He started to stagger towards the man. His feet were unwieldy and uncooperative, causing each step to turn into a stomp, which caused the quarry's yellow dust to mushroom upwards and tickle his nose. He sneezed once.

"You injured pal? You sure look like it. You got to high-tail it over here unless you want them to catch you," the man said. He looked around and started to sort through the rubble and tall grass surrounding him.

"Quick, get over here. I'll look for a branch or something to pull you out of there with. Of all the times to be hanging out in a pit. I just can't believe it."

He continued to wobble over to the wall of earth curving down into the quarry. In a few moments, he reached the embankment. His body felt weak, untested, and heavy. He leaned against the soil with his right shoulder, taking in deep breaths between his heart and stomach. They rattled against his chest. His ribs weren't sure of what was happening. The dirt felt cold and damp against his skin. A gust of wind tickled the back of his head. A few birds chirped.

"Gotta hurry. Gotta hurry," the armored stranger stammered.

He could barely stay awake as he listened. The ground above his tired head was spiked with long weeds. Their shadows were black spear points from the evening sun behind his back. As he looked at their silhouettes, for an eerie second, he heard some voices. Whispers or mumbles, unknown to him, filled his ears. They didn't scare him.

They sounded both familiar and distant.

"Here, I found this," the man suddenly said, breaking the phantom spell. A thick, leafless tree branch dropped down. He stared at it quizzically, grabbing the split-end just below its thickened stalk.

"Hold it good, I'll try to pull you up," he hissed.

13

He tightened his grip. Strangely, the fibrous bark stuck to him, tightening against his skin comfortably. It knew he needed help. How did it know? In a groan from his savior, and a few seconds of panting, he was atop the ledge and looking at the man in the eyes.

"You were way lighter than I imagined. Wow. Or else the apocalypse has made me stronger? My name's Ralph by the way, what should I call you?"

"I, I don't know. I don't know my name."

The man stared at him, blinked, and shook his head.

"You must've been injured or something, that's why you were laying in the middle of the pit with Unnamed wandering around. We can talk more later, you got to follow me. We need to hide for the night."

He wearily trailed the man as they moved silently through the landscape. They were in a rural area. Surrounding them were rows of trees, fields of open grass, and a variety of dirt roads that had a continuous skim of dust hanging over them. It made him think someone had disturbed them recently, even though nobody seemed to be moving. Ralph was the only other person he'd seen since waking up. He wondered if they were all this skinny. Ralph's shoulders and knees poked out from his pants and shirt in boney curls and points. Despite this frailness, he glided noiselessly through each part of the terrain. He followed Ralphs every duck, dash, pause, until his body started to work without a second thought.

"Sometimes they're out during the day. When they are, they're a bit weird. I mean, they're always weird. That's too nice a way to refer to them as. Anyways, they don't really focus on us like they do at night." Ralph said. His voice was hoarse and dry from the clouds of sediment they'd kicked up and fled through.

"What, what are they?" It was difficult for him to shadow Ralph and speak.

"How could you not know at this point? Have you been asleep this entire time?" Ralph said. His voice was quicker and more impatient than before. They weaved across a wide square of green prairie. They reached a line of trees and paused.

"I'm sorry. I don't mean to be short tempered. I'm actually just jealous of your amnesia to be honest. I would be happy to forget the last nine months. I have seen so many horrible things, it is hard to focus on just one to tell you about. I guess the basics is that last April, a drumming sound started playing one evening.

These monsters appeared, and, well, they just started killing everyone without mercy. They're called the Unnamed."

The world seemed to quiet when Ralph said their name. The wind paused. He suddenly could smell Ralph. He was salty and sweaty.

This must be what fear smells like he thought.

Ralph motioned with his shoulder to keep moving. They sprinted through the woods, which opened to a paved road, which was covered in trails of vines and flowers. Without the treetops he finally noticed the sky, which was clear, with a few cauliflower-looking clouds drifting overhead. The twilight of evening had started to sink into the horizon, turning the typical blue into a velvety purple where the heavens touched the earth.

Then he noticed them.

All along the road were a variety of burnt and shattered cars. Minivans, trucks, sedans, tractor trailers, and motorcycles littered the highway in a thick and thorough vehicular graveyard. Glass, metal, and fiberglass caught orange and yellow glints of the impending sunset.

He gawked at them, holding his face with his small hands. His shirt felt tighter and his stomach heavier.

"Yeah, get used to the sight of devastation," Ralph said.

They continued along the road for about a mile. He had a challenging time keeping up with Ralph. Despite his age and piquant appearance, the man moved swiftly between obstacles. They alternated on and off the highway. Occasionally stopping in the ditch for a few minutes while Ralph listened to the world with a tilted neck and tightly closed eyes. Bugs and wind-tossed trees answered back. Ralph would eventually sigh and nod towards the road for them to continue.

"We're getting closer and closer to the drum. If it starts while we're out in the open, expect to stay still for the next 10 hours," he said.

They moved again.

Eventually the woods along their left, parallel to the highway, thinned-out and a building appeared above the treetops. The structure was whitish, black-topped, with a cross in its center. It was smeared over with more vines and flowers like the highway. Ralph dashed for it, expertly jumping over coils of undergrowth. He quickly followed him, crossing a parking lot with a minivan on its side. There were names written in chalk on the charred and rusted roof. He could understand the letters making them. He didn't know how he had that knowledge or skill.

Elena
Gloria
Luke

Ralph suddenly stopped. He looked around wildly, staring at the sky, the ground, and the forest.

"Do you hear that? Do you hear that? The drum has started."

He followed Ralph's motions slightly, listening to the air, craning his head, and pushing his tanned ear to the heavens.

"I, I don't hear anything," he said, solemnly.

"What? How could you not hear it? It is everywhere. It's the sign they're appearing. We need to go hide. Seriously, how could you not hear it? You must have brain damage or gotten hurt or something. You can literally hear it wherever you go. Nothing stops it."

Ralph dashed into the broken, black doors of the building tugging him along with his hand. As Ralph touched him, he felt the ground swell slightly. A low siren filled his brain.

An alarm had been sounded.

The world suddenly lost color. Grays, blacks, and whites replaced the lush scene from before. He blinked a few times and he realized he was standing still, and Ralph was still running ahead of him. There was some sort of stage up ahead with a podium on it. Eyes were staring at him from beneath the platform. Someone suddenly screamed. It was high, long, and from the chest of a child.

How did he know that sound?

He stepped back a second. Ralph stopped and looked at him. He slowly aimed the weapon in his direction. It was a gun. He knew the right word for it now. Color returned to the room. The air stunk of pollen. Bits of dust tickled the evening sunlight coming through the door behind him.

"Wh-what are you?" Ralph said.

He didn't know what to do.

"What are you!?" Ralph said again. He turned to the stage and nodded. "Go hide. I'll take care of this. You're safe."

"Please Ralph," a child whispered.

"Just go!" He barked.

Ralph turned back to him and began to walk slowly into the center of the building. He stopped between the rows of broken benches, which were covered with clusters of rubble. The air grew heavier and stagnant around him. Ralph's eyes had a searing glint to them, they shined in the shadows of the broken room.

16

"Who are you nameless guy? Who are you? What are you?" Something clicked on the weapon he was holding.

"I, I don't know. I don't know."

"Well, I can't kill a nameless man, so I'll give you a name so when I tell this fucked up story to other survivors, in my literal ocean of fucked up stories, they'll know a name." He looked up at the arching roof, which had a hole blown through it. A slant of orange evening light was falling through between curtains of ivy.

"We're in the church of Erasmus, so that'll do, your name is Erasmus now," Ralph said. He tucked the weapon further into his armpit.

"W-wait, I don't even know what's happening or anything. Please. I didn't do anything," he said.

"Look," Ralph snarled.

"L-look? Look at what?"

"Your shadow."

He didn't know exactly what Ralph meant by his shadow. Somewhere in his mind, which had been gripped in an unfamiliar fog since he'd awoken, was a sense of language. Nouns, verbs, adjectives, the very foundations of speech were there. Dust sat frozen in the heavy sunlight. They were trapped by the intensity of the moment. His ears could not hear this drum Ralph mentioned, but he could hear bugs, wind, and the occasional whisper from the shadows. His tongue was heavy and absent with panic. His eyes and neck were sweaty.

What was wrong with his shadow?

The amber slab of dying light was striking Erasmus in such a way his silhouette was highlighted perfectly on the nearby church walls. He didn't know if shadows were supposed to look this way or not, but instead of a normal human outline of shoulders, arms, legs, and a head, there was a tall, tangled mass of spikes, points, and what looked to be horns. It looked ominous and jagged. A nightmare casually followed him. A puppy looking for its mother. The more you tried to explore those details with your vision, the more the penumbra seemed to sink into itself and flex. It was both in motion and standing still.

"I'll say it again, what the hell are you, Erasmus?"

He held up his hands frightened at Ralph.

"I don't, don't know."

"You're clearly one of those Reanimated fuckers, but you don't have a single trace of the Unnamed on you. Not a thread of vine or a bit of discolored skin. I never would have suspected anything."

17

"What, what's Reanimated?"

The wall suddenly crashed inward to his right, throwing plaster, wood, nails, and concrete outwards in a sideways geyser. The immediate cloud of debris blinded him, sending Erasmus backwards. A hulking shape consumed his vision, blocking Ralph, the stage, the podium, and the sun itself. It was dark, flowing, and almost fluid-like. It was twice his size, being both taller and wider than Erasmus's small frame. The only real details he could separate out of this pulsing, fabric mass towering ahead of him, were golden horns or spikes jutting out in jagged points from the entity's shoulders and head.

"No, no, get away!"

There was a rapid popping sound in front of the shape. It was metallic, steamy, and violent. Walls, benches, and the open doors of the church crackled in fragments as bullets bit and tore the building. In seconds, the gun was empty. A smokey, sulfuric fog stung the air. Trickles of debris from the onslaught started to slide down and tinkle onto the ground. The massive shadow shook. Deep in Erasmus's brain a voice suddenly sounded. It was a mixture of animal and human. It was throaty, deep, and struggling to make the connections between letters and sound.

"Run," it said. The raspy gurgle seemed to spring out from the dark mass.

It had wanted to speak for ages.

Erasmus grabbed his head and shook it. Everything was new. He wanted to listen to everything but didn't know anything.

"Run!" It hissed again. The world flexed into a colorless blob from before, a melody played somewhere, and Erasmus's legs turned him towards the door.

He fled.

Outside the church, the world's color snapped back to normal. Erasmus stumbled and panted as he navigated lumps of moss-stained debris. There were lengths of vine spawning across every conceivable path and walkway. He jumped over spikes of rubble mixed-in with the long grass. He did not turn back to look inside the building. There was a crashing sound followed by more gunfire. It echoed out into the silent world, making the empty roads, buildings, forests, and fields around him seem much more infinite, and much more threatening.

Erasmus veered to his right down a roadside ditch, over a creek, and into a patch of woods. He could barely move between the trunks and branches. Behind him the air was quiet, relaxed. The violence from before had turned into memories in a simple second.

18

"What do I do now?" Erasmus said to himself.

He wandered around the woods until the sunlight no longer broke through the branches and leaves. The dark had settled into every pocket and crack of his reality. He kicked stumps and tree roots and sobbed to himself. At one point, he thought he heard yells and screams, but they were distant and almost imaginary. It was hard to trust any of his senses currently, despite his urge to survive.

"What was that back there? Why was Ralph trying to kill me? I don't understand any of it," he said. He started to walk in the direction of the road that sat next to the forest. As he did, lights started to flicker outside the gloom of the woods. Red rays melted in through the underbrush in uneven slices. They looked warm and inviting, but simultaneously made the blackness deeper and vaster.

"Are those streetlights?" Erasmus said, pushing through the brush towards them. How did he know that name? How did he know what they were? He couldn't remember anything about himself, but here he was walking towards something that seemed familiar.

A figure darted across the road, throwing a scuttling silhouette towards Erasmus. A voice sounded somewhere in the back of his mind.

"H-Hello?" He said, approaching the street.

The closer he got to the line of plant-laden pavement; the more Erasmus could see that it wasn't just the streetlights glowing but other objects in the murkiness. Houses, complete with doors, windows, roofs, and lights were lined up. They gave him a memory, the first he really had thus far, of a toy railroad track inside a store, with a small city nestled in and around its plastic veins. He could hear the whirl of the electric tracks pushing it up and down the display.

Then, as easily as it had appeared, the image was gone. His stomach reacted instantly, filling him with a sort of nauseous sadness he'd yet experienced in his short awakening. How could he feel something for a thing he didn't even know existed?

Erasmus stopped just beyond the roadside ditch. It stunk of mud and algae. The black water stole the ghostly glow from the street in a glittering skin. A few bugs buzzed and bounced on the water. They didn't care what was real, and what wasn't.

"Does that look like home to you, you piece of garbage?" A voice snarled somewhere in the trees behind him. It was Ralph. He'd followed him into the woods.

Erasmus dropped to the ground, crawling into the long grass that bordered the forest and narrow wedge of water. The stalks were sharp and tendril-thick, brushing against his sweaty skin, as if they wanted to puncture him, but were too weak.

"I killed that one who jumped in front of you. Your savior or buddy or whatever. It won't be helping you again. It collapsed and was sucked up by the plants." He was closer now, just yards away from him. The luminescence across the road silently darkened in one black wave, leaving just the moon above as the only luminosity. Erasmus smiled about this reaction from the world. He didn't know why.

"That one came so close to killing me and the kids. It was just feet away from finding them. Thank God I had a full clip. Now, stop running, Erasmus. I saw your shadow. You're one of them or something. You can't survive. You just can't."

Erasmus could hear boots breaking the reeds as Ralph approached him. Each step seemed to get bolder. Ralph had known his location for some time.

"I just want to know before I kill you Erasmus, what in god's name are you?"

Erasmus could smell gunpowder again. He covered the back of his head with a pair of trembling hands.

Then, the entire world exploded.

The first physical sensation Erasmus could understand happening around him was that of being pulled, as if he had strings attached to his wrists, ankles, and shoulders. He felt himself carried across the water, pavement, vines, and clusters of debris. Air rushed around him. In mere seconds, he was yanked across the road and up into the tops of a tree. Behind him, Ralph let loose a salvo of bullets into the darkness Erasmus had just been hiding in, peppering the soil in pops of gunpowder.

The gunshots echoed empty and disappointed.

Erasmus was gone before Ralph could really understand what was happening. From Ralph's point-of-view, Erasmus had almost flown away. Ralph spun around and searched the top of the trees across the road for Erasmus. It was full night now, and the moon had dropped behind a cloud, blocking its silver-blue rays from making even the slightest bit of visibility. The air stunk of sour mud, lily pads, and swamp grass. For Ralph, the drum thudded away from some unknown location, shaking the roots of his teeth. For Erasmus, there was the chorus of insects chirping in the deep, and the rolls of the wind hitting the eves.

Erasmus did not know how lucky he was to be ignorant of that apocalyptic thunder.

"You can't run from me you monster. I'll find you. I heard they're assaulting the drum too. They've started to go inside of it. Pretty soon you'll be obsolete. You're just another Reanimated. Another lost puppet of theirs they can't seem to control or understand. You're more alone than anyone in this world, so enjoy that, Erasmus." Before Erasmus could reply he heard some footsteps then silence.

Erasmus had started weeping at some point. How did he know to be sad?

Without the distraction of Ralph's homicidal intentions, Erasmus could finally take full stock of his surroundings. Gone were the feelings of tensions across his limbs. When he had originally been pulled into the eves, he felt a presence on his shoulders. It felt large, hovering, but not necessarily threatening. He carefully tried to turn his body in the branches of the tree to look behind him, but it was gone.

Again, he was alone.

Erasmus carefully descended, using his trembling feet like antennas to feel in the darkness for any sturdy limb to form a ladder. It went easier than he thought, as if the tree was helping him. He reached the ground with relative ease, and slowly approached the silent road. As if programmed on some sort of supernatural cue, the streetlights suddenly illuminated down the street in one glowing row. They formed a friendly orange tunnel beneath the overgrown trees.

Erasmus didn't know why or how he knew, but right there and then, he knew he needed to follow them.

The road twisted through bends of bristled trees for a small eternity. Erasmus walked near the center of the road, occasionally passing crushed cars and tall mounds of broken pavement. Since he'd woken up in that pit, he'd been terrified and worried about almost every new sight and sound. Strangely, all those emotions melted away beneath the streetlights and their phantom power. Erasmus didn't even mind tripping on the cracks in the worn-away highway, which were plentiful. A weak sheet of ice on a winter lake.

The walk stretched on through the most sunken moments of night. Eventually, Erasmus's eyes would wander backwards to see if he was being followed, or if he could identify where he'd started further back on the road. Each time it looked the same; a dark tunnel of trees with a solitary streetlight painting its gloom.

21

"Hard not to stare, isn't it," a voice said from the gloom ahead of him. Erasmus stopped. He'd only been awake a short while, but he was already tired of being frightened at every little thing happening in this desolate world.

"Don't be afraid. The Unnamed are everywhere. If they wanted you dead, you'd be dead. It's as simple as that." The voice said again. It was low, masculine, with a smokiness to it. It was strangely comforting to Erasmus. He didn't know why.

Erasmus could hear footsteps. A man was approaching him. He was dark-skinned, thin, with a goatee and sunken, gaunt face. He was dressed in an orange shirt and jeans, which were baggy and dangling. His mouth turned into a wide smile as Erasmus came into view more.

"Boy am I happy to see you. You're the last one." The man said.

"What, who are you?" Erasmus said, stepping backwards, and nearly tripping on a vine behind him.

Up close Erasmus noticed green vines laced throughout the man's skin. They pushed apart his skin in verdant lines. How did the man live with such open wounds?

"My name is Virgil. Do you have a name yet?"

Erasmus nodded slowly. Something about the name was eerily familiar. He'd heard it before.

"E-Erasmus."

Virgil smiled and pulled his hands away from him and turned around. He pointed at the trees along the streetlights.

"I see. Nice to meet you, Erasmus. We need to hurry before a survivor guns us down. We have a Puppeteer looking over us, but they won't stick around forever. We need to get off the road. You just need to follow me."

"What, what are you saying?"

"Geez, the other ten were right, you do have to be patient for these initial reactions."

Some wind rustled the plants beneath their feet. A few gunshots echoed somewhere.

"The endgame is near Erasmus. The fate of the drum will soon be decided. Whether it survives or not, the Unnamed will be a part of this world. They know it. And they know whatever happens there will be survivors." Virgil said. He started to walk towards the forest parallel to them.

"Would you like to meet your family? If so, follow me."

They continued. Occasionally, Virgil would stop and lightly place his hand on Erasmus's chest. There would be silence, followed by a few twigs and branches cracking. They would duck down to the pavement and sneak behind whatever broken vehicle or miscellaneous rubble was strewn across the road. Each time the echoes grew louder, bolder, a mysterious crescendo of impending violence. It caused Erasmus to constantly scan the dark woods to their left and right.

Whatever was moving, he couldn't see.

"We need to be careful. The Unnamed may not want to harm us, but other Reanimated certainly do. They're jealous, envious, and angry about the more normal looking of the brood. At the onset of all this, well, the Unnamed made mistakes. Things went awry, and now this poor world is left with multiple monsters," Virgil said.

A few raindrops plopped solidly along the leaves and vines beneath their feet. A curl of lightning thrashed across the dark clouds, followed by a groan of thunder. It shook the ground and bounced off the eerie emptiness ahead and behind them. The streetlights suddenly dimmed. Just one stood illuminated above their weary forms.

"The Puppeteer had to move. It doesn't like the weather. Only the hardened ones can make illusions in the rain." Virgil grabbed Erasmus by the hand and pulled him towards the woods along the highway.

"When it rains, the Unnamed are less confrontational because it ruins their camouflage. We can't assume there will be any protection from them in a storm." Virgil yelled. His voice was broken between bits of thunder and rattles of rain.

"What are these things you're even talking about? I don't understand what is happening. One moment I was sleeping, and the next thing I was awake and being chased, whether it was monsters or men." Erasmus said.

"If I tried to completely explain it to you, it would be beyond overwhelming. Best to give you small doses of this living nightmare. I know that's not what you want, but it's what you need."

"How would you know what I need?" Erasmus quickly replied, blowing some raindrops away from his mouth like a horse.

Virgil laughed and rested his back against a tree.

"Fair enough," he said, rubbing his forehead.

Across the road a series of trees suddenly buckled. A large shape, oblong and unbalanced, hobbled through the branches. It was giant, at least ten feet tall, with a wide, muscular build. In the shadows it was difficult to discern any details, but Erasmus could make out what looked like a massive person surrounded by some sort of fleshy padding. Something about them made Erasmus's skin ache. A distant voice started to speak to him from the forest. It almost sounded like a child.

"I'll draw it off. You need to run. Follow the lights when they come back on. Trust them. You have friends in high places. Don't trust humans or Reanimated. They'll all kill you if they can." Wordlessly, Virgil slipped between the trees, jumped over the ditch, and approached the road. He let out a loud yell, which barely rose against the weather and its roar. The monstrous shape sprinted towards him, making the earth shake and bounce as if it was hollow.

All Erasmus could do was watch, then run.

Fleeing, running, and escaping was Erasmus's existence since he'd woken up that evening. He was constantly dodging from one shadow to the next, hiding from whatever abomination had appeared. Worse yet, was the fact that each person he'd interacted with was a stranger, detached from his memory or any prior experience.

Did anyone know him? Was there anyone who he could trust? Ralph had tried to kill him. Virgil had tried to save him. Would there be any common ground? Any consistency?

Erasmus was surprised how many thoughts came to him as he ran through the trees away from the direction of Virgil and that monster. He was getting used to hiding. It seemed to be his purpose in life.

The woods stretched on and on. The trees, leaves, twigs, and branches slashed at him as he ran. Nothing bruised him or broke his skin. They were trying to avoid his sprints or go limp to avoid damaging him. Sometimes he could hear voices coming from the black woods. They were distant, whispered, but there. He wondered if this was supposed to be right? Was it natural? Did everyone hear them?

The foliage thinned and a clearing appeared, dividing the forest. A bit of sky peered down at him. It was dark, black, and star tickled. He stopped to catch his breath. Despite his constant running he wasn't that winded. Erasmus sat down on the grass and stared upwards. Around him was a sort of sweet smell. He didn't know how to compare it to anything, just that it made his mouth water and his eyes heavy. There were no sounds other than a few brushes of wind across the field.

A strange feeling seemed to surround him. There was a heaviness to his shape, like things were being tied to his legs, arms, and shoulders. It reminded him of when he was pulled out of his ditch beneath the barrel of Ralph's gun. This time, the tension was relaxed, non-threatening, like a fishing line with a sleepy angler.

Again, he could feel someone watching him nearby, a form lurking. Then, his senses started to dull, and his mind wandered into a memory. He was in a large room, full of hundreds of people lined up in seats directly ahead of him. There were bright lights. They were trapped suns glaring over him. In his hands was some sort of instrument. He knew what it was but not the name. The people were clapping. The roar of it was loud, but strangely hypnotic. He smiled to himself as it continued.

In seconds, he fell into a peaceful sleep.

It wasn't the morning sun, wind, or dew clinging to his body that woke Erasmus up. Instead, it was the cold, metal nozzle of a gun being jammed into his shoulder blade.

"Wake up. Wake up you monster," a small voice said. Pieces of vines had wrapped around him overnight while he slept. He wrenched at them and panicked. They entangled him just enough to be tight, but not to restrain him. It was a seemingly gentle gesture. They wanted Erasmus to know he was not a prisoner nor a target. It felt kind to him. He didn't know why.

"Get up you, you goddamn piece of shit," the voice said. Erasmus felt the cold front of the weapon jab into his arm, knocking him back onto his knees. The person speaking sounded wavering and scared. They weren't sure of the threats they were supposed to be invoking.

"I-I'm trying to, if you let me stand, I'll get up," Erasmus said, raising his hands.

"I'll shoot you right here!" They screamed.

Erasmus finally stood up and blocked out the sun with a shaking hand to stare at the figure. It was a little girl, about 10 years old, with red hair, powdery skin, and black glasses, which were missing one lens and had patches of duct tape wrapped around them in uneven coils. She was wearing a brown hooded sweatshirt, with some sort of utility belt wrapped around her shoulder. Various bullets, a flashlight, and a small knife were attached to it. She was wearing jeans, pink tennis shoes, and had her hair tied back in a ponytail. Her entire appearance seemed dirty, as if every fleck and speck of this apocalypse had stuck to her sweaty body at some point.

"Who are you?" Erasmus said with a surprisingly low snarl. He was getting tired of asking these questions. Would he ever not be someone's prey in this new reality?

"My name is Elena. And you killed Ralph. I'm here to make it right." She said, pointing her rifle at him.

"I didn't kill anyone. I just woke up. This entire time things have been trying to kill me. This. Entire. Time. I can't find any peace. I don't want to hurt anyone." He was tired of constantly being chased, hunted, and accused. He walked away from Elena's shaking form. He rubbed his small forehead, disinterested in whatever gripe or animosity she had. He headed through the clearing he'd just slept in, navigating the long grass brushing against his knees.

"Where are you going? I'm, I'm talking to you!"

Erasmus didn't respond. He plodded ahead. In front of him was a strip of trees with a road running parallel to it. He would go through the forest and follow the road wherever it would lead him, regardless of monsters or people.

"It is not my fault. I just woke up. I don't even know my real name. It's not my fault," Erasmus mumbled to himself.

The gun fired behind him suddenly. There was a violent pop, followed by a whistle. The ground shuttered, causing Erasmus to nearly trip. A shadow formed behind him, pushing the sunlight away and throwing a dark sheet over him. He turned around to find what could only be described as a golden fin slicing out of the ground. It was tall, about eight feet high, and curved. There were vertical lines rising along it, with threads of green vines weaved throughout them. Erasmus noticed a few cracks along the material. It was made of soft, but flexible glass.

"No!" Elena screamed. More gunfire cut through the air. The amber shield vibrated and snapped under the bullets. Her weapon clicked empty after a few seconds. The shield seemed to grumble and turn towards her. Erasmus tried to focus on where the shape was jutting loose from the soil, but whatever it was attached to was obscured by the sediment.

It started to move towards Elena.

"No. No. Get away. Get away from me!"

The gold fin continued to approach her. The ground surrounding where the thin object pierced the dirt was trembling and shifting. The very earth itself was afraid of what disturbed it.

"I can't let it mark me. I can't. I can't."

The fin followed noiselessly. Despite the bullets and the rage dripping out of Elena, Erasmus did not want anything to happen to her. She was a small child. Something in his fractured identity made him uneasy about her being harmed. He reached a trembling hand out into the air behind the shape.

26

"Please, let, let her go," Erasmus said.

There was a hiss somewhere. The wind settled. The trees, grass, and sky seemed to freeze. The black and white returned to his vision. Only the fin had any color, still glowing a nearly translucent yellow in the surrounding opaque scene. Then, reality flashed back. The plate descended silently, dropping just below Elena's trembling feet. Erasmus suddenly felt exhausted and staggered backwards. He sat down quickly to avoid fainting. The wet morning grass soaked his pants. A headache began throbbing above his eyes. He closed them and rested his forehead against his arms.

"Um, what did you just do?" Elena said. She wanted to run and hide. She had spent plenty of time around monsters, and she knew that one was always followed by others.

Erasmus shook his head.

"I don't know. I just asked it to stop."

"I've heard plenty of people try to speak to the Unnamed. Usually, they're begging them for their lives. They've never listened. In fact, that usually just makes them die faster, like the monsters take offense to it or something."

She started to approach him again.

"I don't know whether to run or say thank you."

"Say whatever you want. I just don't want to see anyone getting hurt or killed. Since I woke up in that pit all I've been surrounded by are monsters and madness." Erasmus said. His head still throbbed. His vision was blurry. "I don't want to get blamed for anything."

Elena sighed.

"Ralph said you were one of them. The Unnamed or a Reanimated. He said you were dangerous. He told me and the others that too."

She swallowed a few tears.

"It wouldn't have been the first time he was wrong though."

Elena extended her small hand. It was still shaking from the bullets she'd fired.

"My name is Elena," she said.

Erasmus extended his hand, and for the first time that he could remember or knew of, a tight smile spawned across his thin face.

"It is nice to meet you," he said.

When Erasmus shook Elena's small hand, he noticed how raw, soft, and barely together her skin felt. It was almost like he was touching a toy. A collage of strange images jumped in front of his visible reality. They weren't Erasmus, but of her at different

27

locations throughout the countryside. The many perspectives were from the rooftops, behind trees, and in an empty house with people screaming.

Who was chasing her? Why could he see it suddenly?

"You can let go of my hand now," she said with a tight grimace. Erasmus quickly pulled his arm back. He was immediately embarrassed, tucking his shoulders over his chest and holding his hands up.

"Sorry."

"It's okay. You must be a Reanimated. Ralph said the first ones that appeared acted like they'd never talked to a real person before. That was until they turned and started to change. That was until they wanted to kill us too," she said, blocking out the sun with a dirty sleeve.

"It's getting hot, can we go in the shade?" Elena moved towards the line of trees billowing and rustling behind Erasmus. He followed gingerly, staring at the ground, and looking for signs of the fin.

"Aren't you worried about what just appeared?"

"If that thing wanted me dead, I would be. Again, the Unnamed never show mercy." Elena mumbled without looking away from the tree line. They reached the tangled wall of branches. Elena slid into them expertly; her thin, small frame parting them without causing a single tremble in the undergrowth. She led them a little deeper into the woods, where the air stunk of cold soil and bark. They stopped at a toppled birch tree and sat down atop its white, cloven trunk. Erasmus stared at the flakey, obsidian shapes dotted across its papery surface. They were black, eye-like, like someone had sketched a pupil into them with a living charcoal. Erasmus couldn't stop staring at them.

"What is the Reanimated?" He said, sitting down next to her. She pulled a green canteen out and took a quick drink. Her throat thumped as she drank. He got jealous. He didn't know why.

"How much do you want me to tell you?" She said, offering the bottle to Erasmus.

"I'm good. Not thirsty."

"Seriously? It is so hot out here."

"I haven't felt thirsty or hungry since I woke up."

"Must be nice," Elena said, pulling her gun around onto her lap. She started to fidget with the chamber. The weapon looked bulky and somewhat obscene against her body. It was like the two images themselves were clashing. Erasmus could feel the irony as he looked at them, but it was hard for him to describe it. He just felt it was wrong.

"The Reanimated appeared after the Unnamed, which came with the drum," she said, not looking up. She began to clean the chamber with an oily rag she'd just pulled from her pocket.

"Which one is which?"

"The Unnamed are what appeared in the church when Ralph freaked out at you, and in the ground just now too. They're like these shadowy, skeleton things that appear when the drum starts. They have different forms, like that one in the ground between us just now. The Reanimated appear as people at first, but then they start going crazy and turning into these giant monsters."

"So, what made the Reanimated?"

"The Unnamed actually, after they kill us, they harvest our parts and recreate people all sewn together. We're sort of like dolls."

"My god, and I'm one of those," he said, astonished.

"A Reanimated? I think so, though I've never seen the Unnamed get along or protect one like what just happened.

"So, what made the Unnamed?"

Elena laughed and flipped her gun over. She played with a lever on it, and something snapped. She wiped away a few tears from her eyes and blinked violently. Erasmus couldn't tell if she was happy or sad.

"That is the million-dollar question, isn't it?"

An eerie silence seemed to hold the world around them.

"So, I was made by monsters?" Erasmus said, unclenching and clenching his small fists while staring at the leaf-marbled forest floor. He was still fighting the panic coursing through his body. He had not felt much pain and want in his Reanimated shell, but the fear of his origin outweighed any supernatural boundaries to discomfort.

"Yes," Elena said quickly and emphatically, standing and testing the gun by pushing it into her small shoulder. Sweat was forming on her forehead. She wiped it casually. Erasmus felt his own. Still no sweat.

"Maybe we can find a few around to show you. Sometimes in the woods, the ones that don't hide when the drum starts just sort of stand around. They become almost like statues. They won't harm you unless they notice you. Like, really notice you. It's weird, but everything's weird. I mean it's the end of the world," she said. She started to walk briskly. Erasmus let out a groan and followed immediately.

How many more tours through this hell was he going to get?

As Erasmus followed her, he could feel parts of the earth rising behind him. The fin from before was following them, tracking his footsteps. It was there to help him, but ready to kill her. Why was he in-between? Why was his life coming at the potential expense of others?

"Ha! I knew they'd be here. They always come back to the same spot during the day. I see a few up ahead," Elena suddenly said.

"W-what?" Erasmus said, trying to convince his brain to get back to reality.

"The Unnamed, remember. You wanted to see a few. I said during the day they are docile, or that's what Ralph said. I don't even know what the word means. Anyways, there are a few up ahead."

Elena stopped and stared at Erasmus.

"God, look at that? Not a single mosquito wants you. It's true what they say about you Reanimated. The bugs don't bother you."

Erasmus didn't say anything.

"Do I have to teach you what bugs are too?"

"So, I don't have to worry about them?" Erasmus said, nodding ahead, and ignoring her condescending tone. Through the spaces between the many trunks, he could see two shapes up ahead. They were tall, unmoving, and wide.

"No, not right now unless you shoot them with a gun or something. During the day they're so disgustingly peaceful. At night when the drum sounds, they hunt us nonstop. Also, I think these ones are wounded, or messed up, or something. The ones that get shot at and survive usually don't hunt at night."

Elena shook her head and whispered.

"They're damaged goods, just like the rest of us."

Erasmus didn't want to look scared of what stood ahead of him. Whatever they were, they still sat obscured by a cluster of silent trees. He tried to hide his physical reaction to seeing them. His small frame shook from his narrow shoulders down to his thin legs. His shirt, shorts, and parts of his shoes had already been torn and slashed by his various escapes and dashes through the never-ending woodlands. His skin, which was tan, but had hints of green beneath its layers, would be sweating wildly if he was biologically capable of it. His short black hair felt heavy. His small face was unsure of which expression to form.

"Are you sure it's safe?"

"For you, yeah, but probably not for me. Just don't do anything stupid to wake them up or anything."

A crow cackled somewhere. Erasmus thought he heard voices behind it.

"I just want you to see where you came from," Elena said.

"Why?"

"So, you know why I acted the way I did. So, you know why I tried to kill you. I feel bad about it."

Elena stopped.

"They're right up ahead. I'm going to stay back." Her gun was shaking with nervousness. She refused to look at him as he walked by. She nodded tightly, almost solemnly, and melted back into the forest.

Ahead, the tree trunks thinned out into a small clearing. The canopy broke apart as well, letting loose another slab of sunlight, which was tickled by more bits of dust and cobwebs. Standing ahead of Erasmus were two large, nearly 10-foot shapes, hunched over the ground, as if they were almost praying into the green floor.

The more Erasmus looked at them, the more time seemed to pause. His muscles tightened up. His back grew sore. He felt like he was being watched by something, but he couldn't figure out where, or how, or even, when. The more he stared at the Unnamed, the more vague details he could make out about their thoroughly menacing bodies. They were wrapped in a fluctuating cloak, which was beyond dark and shadowy. It was the deepest obsidian you could ever carve out from the earth. Despite their abyssal shape, Erasmus could still find intricate details peering back at him from their forms. There were bits of greenery webbed throughout their body. Vines, flowers, and rib-like branches were poking out at random points. Nature was living inside of them, and their growth would not be denied, not even by their nightmarish properties. There was no face, just a hood, which had gold horns protruding upwards and sideways from its head. Other than the basic outline of a human being, with shoulders and a back, there were not many other details from Erasmus's vantage point.

Except for the hands, if you could even call them that.

Dangling at their sides were a pair of obscene golden claws, which were a cross between icicles and curved blades. They were nearly the size of Erasmus, and were encrusted with red veins, which were scribbled in patterns and breaks. It was a language no human knew. The points of these killing extensions were jammed into the ground. Along their backs were more of these golden horns and points, which spiked out in random bursts. Crows were sitting atop them peacefully. They casually turned their heads to look at Erasmus then flew away. They scattered upwards in caws and inky flaps.

Then, the Unnamed moved.

It was hard to tell what the Unnamed were exactly doing. They were standing up but didn't seem to really have legs. Their bodies turned towards Erasmus slowly. The earth beneath their shadowed forms wasn't moving, but they were, fluctuating in and out of reality. There were voices sneaking into Erasmus's ears. They whispered and mumbled.

Without any will of his own, Erasmus began to walk towards them. He didn't know why. He didn't even want to know. He just needed to see them closer. They had a gravity, a pull, a phantom heaviness that convinced secret forces to power his unnatural DNA to move, to follow, and to listen. One of the Unnamed stopped moving, and resettled its large claws into the dirt, seemingly uninterested about Erasmus's presence.

The other Unnamed continued to turn towards him, pulling itself free of the forest floor effortlessly; without disturbing a single leaf or twig. There was a slight hiss from the creature. The deep, almost acrid stench of fresh soil filled the air, as it parted from the layers of greenery. The Unnamed towered over Erasmus. Before he could take full stock of its appearance, its ribs, which were gold, boney, and open to the world, floated directly ahead of him. In another hiss, higher and more violent than the one before, they broke apart. Something in Erasmus's memories triggered. He'd seen these ribs open before. He didn't know where. He didn't know how.

Then, they were around him, enveloping him like the closing petals of a flower, only they weren't some delicate living lace, but a hardened, fibrous bone, which gleamed with viscous bronze. A sweet smell surrounded him as well. His mouth watered strangely; it was a new sensation. Since he'd woken up in his pit, he hadn't been hungry or thirsty.

Erasmus wanted to move. He wanted to run, but there was something so certain about the ribs. They weren't moving violently, or with some sort of clawed malice. They were gentle, calm, as if they were trying to embrace him. In mere seconds, they were wrapped around him. He felt himself being pulled towards the Unnamed. Ahead of him, daylight, the green of the forest, and any other image vanished. The smells and sounds disappeared as well. Gone were the brushing of wind on eves and the bold wetness of the woodland. There was only darkness everywhere. He found himself floating it in. He felt underwater, even though he had never swum before. Erasmus started to panic, but his limbs were distant in his mind. They didn't feel attached anymore.

Then, he heard it.

Someone was singing nearby in the void. It was small, soft, and soothing. It was a lullaby, just for him.

So many images appeared then vaporized across Erasmus's dreamy vision while the Unnamed had him in its golden cage of ribs and spectral sinews.

The first was of what looked like a black aircraft hovering over a huge body of water. It looked strange, yet familiar, like he had seen it before, but a different version of it. The ship was flat, black, with two long wings and a round center. It flew effortlessly, glowing with engine fire but not emitting a sound crushing boom. It paused over some water, and what looked like a black seed dropped into the water unceremoniously. Then, the plane of sorts banked right and spun upwards into the clouds without a second thought or hesitation.

Next, the image was a shoreline of sand, seaweed, and small waves beneath blinding sunlight. Then it began to shutter, like an internal antenna needed to be adjusted inside his brain. Out in shallows a feminine shape with green tendrils swam, bending and twisting in the teal surf as if she were a freed prisoner. She dived into the darkness after a few laps back and forth. A few shadows followed her out to the deeper blue. They were larger, and somewhat muddled in their silhouettes. They almost looked like overturned ships.

As these visions passed before Erasmus, there were no smells or sounds. The trance was eerily silent causing him to hear his own impatient breath gasping, and the occasional sound of foliage being brushed or snapped from outside the monster's moving bones. Despite the obvious physical movement of the monster around Erasmus's body, which was curled into a ball within this bronze prison, his form did not move. He was suspended, almost cradled.

He hadn't felt this safe since he'd been alive.

The last vision was the most abstract. It was a huge forest, larger than anything Erasmus had in his broken memories, overlooking empty plains of grass and flowers. The trees were massive, stretching into the sky and spreading out in jade patterns. They reminded Erasmus of tall buildings and a winding train worming through their skyscraper bellies. He didn't know why he had that memory for comparison. He didn't know where it came from.

Then, the movement stopped. There was the clatter of gunfire, followed by desperate yells and quick explosions. These sounds were becoming a pattern to Erasmus's very existence. A violent echo following him through every setting he came across. Was the universe constantly set ablaze by malice and war? Or was it just him? Was he cursed with some sort of breathing, bullet-wild requiem?

Erasmus seemed to be floating inside the Unnamed. His stomach felt light. Air rushed by him through gaps in the monster's skeleton. Then, there was a collision of dirt, plant, and his flesh.

And then there was again, silence.

Erasmus was covered by something. His body couldn't really feel or understand what it was or how it was attached to him. It was damp, stringy, and tough. It hung on his limbs as he stirred. His body felt numb, achy, as if he had been stuck sleeping in the same position for years. It took minutes for him to break his head free of what was strangling him. He writhed and tore against himself, feeling parts of the botanical bonds around him start giving way.

"Is that someone down there?" A young, feminine voice chimed from the darkness. Erasmus couldn't really see anything except for a tangled mass of what appeared to be vines webbed across his face. He bit into it with his teeth in panic, tasting soil and blood from his gums. Strangely, the plants scattered away from him quickly as he gestured towards them. Erasmus fell forward and onto the ground in a tumble. His shoulders and back cracked and snapped. His body wanted to send out sensations of pain. The human parts of it cried out in agony and panic, but the supernatural vines from the drum which held his DNA together made those sensations die before the neurons of his remade brain could absorb them.

Erasmus looked upwards from the point of his thrashing descent. There was a knot of vines above his head, tangled and weaved into some sort of corded sun. A gust of wind shook it, and it seemed to pulse like some sort of tethered heart. It fell apart in a collapse of brown dust, sprinkling across Erasmus in brackish rain. Beyond the vanished conflux of vines was a standard forest canopy with a sunny blue sky.

"What? Where am I?"

It had been the question; bullying him, torturing him, and stalking him since he woke up in the pit.

"Did you hear that? Someone's down here. Is the area clear? I thought it was," the voice said. Erasmus started to stagger through the trees towards where they thinned out and the daylight was glaring through in white chunks. A few flies buzzed by. A moth ascended on sunbeams.

Two people approached Erasmus. One was male, older, and curled into a question mark. He was covered in gray body armor, which had a whole map of abuse scratched and torn throughout it. Chest, shoulders, forearms, all showed signs of slashes and cuts. The man had the same abrasions on his sunken face, with non-existent teeth, and a wispy smear of sable hair. He was holding some sort of gun, but Erasmus couldn't tell what it was. Next to him was a tall strawberry blond woman, with soft blue eyes and flat nose, light skin, and tight lips that signaled a constant state of consternation. She was dressed in similar fatigues. There was something about her presence that made Erasmus feel both scared and familiar. He had seen her before, but he didn't know when. His body could barely work. His mind needed time to catch up with reality. For Erasmus it was a chase with no ending mark.

"Oh my god. It can't be? It can't," the woman suddenly said.

Erasmus looked at her again. He suddenly became self-conscious and felt the material of his flannel shirt and his khaki shorts nervously with his fingertips. This was a new mannerism in the hall of weirdness that was his unknown identity. The clothing felt different. It was extra thin, weathered, as if it had been exposed to unchecked elements. The woman stood motionless. The breeze buckled the trees around them. The old man looked at her quizzically with a crooked chin and scrunched face.

"Um, do I know you?" Erasmus finally said.

She took a deep breath.

"You don't recognize me, Erasmus?"

Another pause.

"I guess I'm not surprised you don't recognize me. It has only been twelve years." The woman lowered her weapon and nodded at the old man who copied her gesture.

"It's okay Ron, he's a friend. An old friend, but a friend nonetheless."

"What? Is this the one you talked about? The one that vanished?" Ron said, in a throaty, deep voice. Erasmus noticed his body shaking when he talked. In fact, he had tremors. It would wander to his arms, shoulders, and head.

"Yup. Never thought I'd see him again after that Unnamed gobbled him up and jumped into the ground. I thought my mind was playing tricks on me."

"Well, that's easy enough, Elena, in this bizarre world of ours." Ron replied.

Erasmus looked at the woman a bit closer. He remembered the name instantly. It felt like just seconds ago the Unnamed was wrapping its ribs around his body, showing him the shore with teal water, and the skyscraper-sized trees.

"I think he's getting it," Elena said. She trotted down the ditch, which curved downwards into the woods.

"I was, I was only gone a few moments it seemed like. How did this happen?" Erasmus said, staring at the woman. His voice was dry. The words barely squeaked out.

"It's a good question, I'm afraid there aren't many, if any answers though," Elena said with a grimace. She walked up to look at him. "Yup, other than your clothes looking a little worse for wear, you haven't aged a day."

"I don't think I've seen a Reanimated as perfect as him," Ron said, carefully walking down the muddy incline, using a few birch trees to balance. A dog followed him. It was a chocolate lab, with long brown hair and a red collar. It barked and dashed down to where Erasmus stood.

"Buffy. Buffy. You take it easy," Ron said, sternly.

The dog pushed against Erasmus, nuzzling its nose and forehead under his right hand. It whined and cried like it had not received human contact in forever.

"Right Buffy, is life so hard? Dogs love the Reanimated," Elena said. She unlatched a canteen from her vest and by reflex handed it to Erasmus, but then stopped. "Sorry, I forgot you don't need stuff like this."

Erasmus started to scratch the dog's snout, which caused its bushy tail to thwack the back of his legs. He started to cry. More puzzles. More enigmas. Would his life ever have any clarity?

Elena walked over to him and put a hand on his trembling shoulder.

"I'm sorry. I knew things were shocking before, but this must just be awful. At least you didn't miss much the last 11 years, other than the drum being destroyed," she said.

"The drum is gone?"

"Oh yes, shortly after you disappeared a group of people snuck inside and destroyed it. A huge forest formed in the center of the country. We're about to head in that direction, but a few rogue Unnamed had been reported in the area."

Erasmus stared at her astonished and coughed nervously.

"A huge forest you say?"

Erasmus and Elena stared at each other for a few seconds. Afternoon sun made the forest light heavy and sleepy. Wind billowed a little bit of everything. The mixed smells of moss, dirt, and rock formed an earthy aroma all around them.

"Yeah, after the drum was destroyed, most of the Unnamed and Reanimated headed for the continental divide. Turns out a huge forest had sort of grown there during the drum. They called it the Jade, because, well, it's bright green." She walked in small circles inspecting Erasmus. She stopped and looked back at Ron.

"It's really him."

"Wow, has he changed at all?" Ron said, picking his way through the trees towards their small clearing. He wasn't as fluid or sure on his feet as Elena. Erasmus had never seen a human as old as him before. He couldn't help but stare at him.

"The Drum got destroyed?" Erasmus said, again struggling to talk. If he had been asleep for 11 years, even his supernatural body would need some time to adjust.

"Yeah, sure did, thankfully. The Unnamed are still dangerous, but they don't try to murder us every waking moment. In fact, the ones in the Jade are absolutely vicious. We were asked by our Bureau to head that direction with a bunch of other volunteers to help secure an outpost in Old Colorado, near the northern tip of the Jade."

"Yes, asked is a nice word for it." Ron mumbled.

"So, the Unnamed aren't gone?"

"No, if only. They're just as terrifying, but not enough to want to kill us if we cross paths with them under unsavory conditions. They're more like wild animals. Usually, they don't bother you unless they're threatened. Of course, next to the Jade it is a different story, which is why we're walking there right now." Elena said.

She again walked up to Erasmus and put her hand on his back. "How do you know about it, old friend?"

Erasmus found the kindness odd considering she wanted to kill him originally. Things must be different now somewhat. Something must have changed since that night when he woke up in the gravel pit.

"I saw it when I was inside the Unnamed. That, and some sort of ocean and shore. But there was a forest for certain."

37

"Sounds like you're the perfect guy to bring along with us. Elena said you could talk to the Unnamed too. You saved her life. Now, that was some time ago, but you'll get your shot again with where you're going," Ron said.

Elena wrapped her arm around his shoulders and nodded with a sly, tight smile.

"Yeah, sounds like a match made in heaven," she laughed.

Erasmus looked back and forth at the two of them.

"Do I have a choice?"

Things had both changed and stayed the same since Erasmus had been asleep in the chest of that Unnamed.

The landscape they walked through was like when he was asleep. There were long country roads with unending curves and hills. The sky was a blue slab that pushed onto the earth with uncensored heat and dryness. The green of nature was lush and extreme everywhere you looked. Trees were overburdened, grasses were long and bristled, and wildflowers billowed amongst the prairie glass in lace jewels. Bumblebees constantly brushed and bumped into their emblazoned discs in an awkward, yet charming feeding-frenzy.

The roads no longer had the mechanical skeletons of burnt-out automobiles. They had been dragged to the side and dropped into the ditch. They were nothing more than rusty memories, craned and bowing to a world they used to belong to. The pavement they walked on had weeds in every crack and blemish. They were borderline unusable, but still vehicles would pass them by, preceded by engine grumbles and the honks of their horns. In their wake would be a dirt-colored cloud of stinging exhaust that Erasmus couldn't really smell but made his eyes water.

"Not a whole lot has changed since your nap, old boy," Ron said, ambling along.

"Yeah, I suppose after 11 years you might expect things to be a little different. Well, when about 82 percent of humanity is wiped out in the course of about a year, reestablishing anything vaguely civilized is pretty hard." Elena said, walking ahead of him.

"We just started to get fed regularly in the last few years. Food was scarce for survivors, especially with the Unnamed destroying it at the end. Took five years to get the power grid working again too, even now it's still fragmented."

"Took more like 4 and half years," Ron interjected.

"Sorry, my mistake, Ronald." Elena said with an eye roll. She stared at Erasmus and rolled her eyes. "He's all protective of it. He worked on it after all."

38

"So how do we get around? How do we make it to this place if it's half a country away?" Erasmus asked. He was feeling a little bit calmer about everything, knowing he wasn't being hunted or attacked like he was for that first night of reality. Still, when they passed by other survivors, all of whom were dressed in body armor and armed like Ron and Elena, he couldn't help but feel out of place. Elena noticed his long stares and awkward eyes into the dirt as they passed a cluster of people on the opposite side of the road.

"Don't worry about being recognized or attacked. You're one of those human-looking Reanimated. You're realistic, not some bloody green mannequin. Most people won't bat a second eye at you. Just try and look normal, and act normal, too. We're okay around here. Ron and I are well known in this area. The closer we get to the west though, the smarter you'll have to be," she said.

They stopped underneath a bulbous tree for some shade and water. Erasmus forced some down his throat in the effort to appear human. Elena nodded her head in approval and wiped the sweat from her brow with a red handkerchief. The heat was oppressive, it hung over the road like an apparition. Elena drained the rest of the green canteen she'd just shared and coughed.

"To answer your earlier question about travel, well, most of it will be walking once we get close to the Jade. You can't drive any cars, planes, or anything within a few hundred or so miles of the Jade, unless you want the Unnamed breathing down your neck. We'll be taking a train to one of the outpost cities, then walking in from there."

"It'll be a long trip, you'll need a book," Ron said.

Erasmus looked at him with a mixture of both astonishment and embarrassment.

"I don't know how to read." He whispered.

Eventually, Erasmus, Ron, and Elena reached a small town sitting off the road, wrapped, and divided in dirt streets and faded stop signs. The buildings were strange for Erasmus. He didn't have much of a reference point in his Reanimated mind. There were no real structures when he woke up in that pit. Only the church where he was almost killed was the only echo back to civilization before the drum and Unnamed. In his broken memories he could see teeming, tall cities with rows of concrete and metal.

They weren't his though. He didn't know where they came from.

This town was a rusty echo to those great skyscraper accomplishments planted in Erasmus's mind. These structures were a hodgepodge of found and scavenged materials. There was brick, metal, fabric, wood and even a bright foam of blue or pink fused among the rooftops, walls, and various other spots. The village looked sewn together, like the apocalypse had leveled everything, but instead of having the infrastructure to recreate it, there was only rubble to build back with.

Nothing stood higher than three stories. Solar panels and windmills beamed and stirred amongst their bulging walls. There were dozens of tables and chairs outside each porch, front door, and entryway, where people smoked, drank coffee, and chatted. The air was hot and dusty. A sweet, but stinging smell of tobacco hovered over the crowds. The general hubbub of the city and ache of various vehicles pushing their ancient motors drowned out Erasmus's anxious thoughts.

He was happy not to be crushed by the silence of fear, or the constantly rustling forests and fields which had followed him since his awakening.

Ron wobbled through the masses to a table underneath a slight overhang in the shade. He waved at a few acquaintances, then motioned Erasmus to follow him. Elena stayed close behind, with her weapon drawn. The whole throng had guns draped over their shoulders, backs, and tucked into their belts. The sun reflected an endless gunpowder glint.

Erasmus felt both safe and endangered.

"Take a seat, bud. I'm going to get us some coffee," Ron said, pointing at the table. He wandered through the crowd into the building. Elena sat down next to him. It was a round, wooden surface with a variety of scratches and dents. A half full ashtray sat in its center still smoking. Elena grabbed the butt and inspected it with one eye before taking a quick drag.

"I thought you had glasses?" Erasmus said, watching her.

"I did, but they broke long ago, and I haven't been able to afford them since." She said, pushing back in her chair. It wobbled, but she didn't seem to care. The entire world didn't seem to be sitting right.

"So how did you find those Unnamed? Or me for all that matter?" Erasmus asked.

Elena dropped the butt back into the center and looked around.

"Ron is taking forever with that coffee." She fidgeted a bit, then put her weapon on the table in a metal thud. She let her hair down then scooped it up quickly, retying it into a taunt ponytail. Her skin looked a little dirty, and sunburnt, but overall, she looked healthy.

"We were out on a bounty for a few Unnamed. They had been sighted just outside of town. Apparently, they had been buried in the forest and sort of just woke up. We weren't expecting to kill them, the bounty was just for reconnaissance. Like I said earlier, not all the Unnamed are out to kill us. If we can avoid conflict, we do it. Takes too many bullets. Anyways, when we approached them, they sort of walked up to us, and charged, but it was half-hearted. We didn't even want to kill them, but we couldn't take that chance. We dropped one after a quick spray, but the second one fled and collapsed into the trees just below that ravine. It just sat there with its back to us and let us kill it. I have never seen that before. Then, below it, there you were, a dazed and confused ghost from a decade ago," she said.

Elena had pulled off her backpack when she sat down. She rummaged through it suddenly looking for something. Ron reappeared with three cups of coffee. The steaming liquid was in three different mugs of varying sizes and colors. Erasmus had noticed how eclectic the world had become since his sleep. Life was sort of mashed together, no matter how small or large it was.

"Here, here it is." Elena said, setting down a brown, leather-bound book in the center of the table. "This will have many of your answers for what happened."

Ron nodded and swung around a chair and sat down.

"Ah yes, the Greenland Diaries."

Key Largo: 01

When the drum first started, neither sister wanted to do anything but hide.

It was easier that way. They'd watched a few other survivors try to fight the monsters wandering the shadows with their guns and bullets, but every time the shapes would simply shrug off their attacks and dive into their bodies with their claws, until the earth below their bloody feet was carved out with their bone and bile. The people would scream words at first, but it would go wild and liquid as their flesh came apart. Most of the time the girls watched people die at night. They were lucky to have the dark blot out the gory details. The sounds of their demises still echoed in their girl's nightmares though, which had dominion with or without the drum.

The girls were on vacation in Florida with their family when the apocalypse hit. Their parents loved the Sunshine State. It was their favorite place to take their kids. Now that the girls were older, Disney World and Universal Studios were echoes of their adolescent past. They were more interested in getting the perfect tan, taking pictures of the lagoon outside their hotel, and sneaking sips of liquor off extra drinks their parents would order. Key Largo was the perfect spot for them. It was picturesque; emerald-tickled water with flour-white sand, craning palm trees with jade leaves, and turning waves that never rolled high with frothy violence. You were living in a postcard you'd find spinning in a metal rack in the corner of a gift shop.

Then the drum came, and even though the beach maintained its natural beauty from the explosion of greenery, the ripped apart cars and buildings, and the streaks of devastation along the highway down the keys made both Hilda and Freya tired of this forsaken paradise.

"Why do you think mom yelled your name first when it happened?" Hilda asked her sister. They were sitting on some lawn chairs behind the hotel on the sand, facing the turquoise bay. The chairs were permanently fused to the ground by vines and flowers, despite them sitting on a bed of sediment. The entire natural world had been turned upside-down when the drum happened.

"What? When?" Freya replied. She was in a pair of shorts and a pink shirt. She was blond and blue-eyed, just like her older sister. Their parents were Norwegian. They were four years apart but often people thought they were identical twins.

"You know when, when the sound happened, and the monsters showed up. They came bursting through every door, one-by-one, until they reached us. Then mom yelled your name to run, and I just did, and we jumped off the balcony and hid in the palm trees next to us," Hilda said.

"Oh, I see. I don't know. She was playing cards with me. I was right in front of her. She just said my name."

Hilda stood up and placed her hands on her hips. She was wearing black tights with a green top. The skin on her feet was covered in bug bites. She was warm but trying to protect herself from the Florida sun. The heat of the summer hadn't gone away with the rest of civilization.

"Just curious," she said, letting her hair down to tie into a more complete ponytail.

"No more of this favoritism, Hilda? You know they loved us both the same. She just said my name because I was there," Freya said, standing up.

"I didn't say that. When did I say that." Hilda said, walking down the beach. The shadow of the hotel was looming over them. It was a square building with white siding and balconies like vertebrae. Every window was shattered. There might be more shards of glass than there were grains of sand.

"Besides, she's dead anyways," Freya said, following her.

"We need to hide. It'll start soon. She'll be coming out. Where do you want to go today?" Hilda said.

"Anywhere but the dumpsters."

Key Largo: 02

Brandon wasn't equipped to deal with an apocalypse, but who was?

He couldn't believe it was actually happening. It had been weeks since it all started. There was the haunting thunder, the shapes, and the echo of their living blades against the walls. His parents were killed on the first night. Brandon was lucky enough to be buried inside the bathroom under a pile of ceramic rubble as they attacked. Afterwards, the world collapsed in mere days and the road through Key Largo was a sideways skeleton of civilization. Vacation had been switched for survival. A trivia category on some sort of game show. The walls of the condo smelled of blood. The air outside had a stench of oil to it. Fires were burning with no one to put them out. Worse yet, the entire world was eerily silent if you wandered away from the bending waves of the beach.

Brandon was large for eighth grade. He was nearly six feet tall, with pale skin that dodged the sunlight, but embraced the pixilated glow of an HDMI cord. He had long black hair, a round face, and permanent frown, which was there before the monsters appeared. His forehead had a small galaxy of acne, a superficial concern that was lost against the lack of running water, power, heat, and living shadows. He wore the same clothes from that night in the bathroom. A black shirt with a faded Ren and Stimpy image, gray shorts, and a pair of red sandals with white socks, which were now black from debris and dirt. He had other clothes that his mom packed for their vacation, but he didn't want to change.

Being in the same outfit of that night reminded him of his family.

There was nothing left to bury when the creatures came through those doors. All he could do was cry and talk to memories of his family next to the emerald beach. The water was still beautiful against all the devastation. It reminded him of a heaven he hoped his parents were in.

After a while, Brandon had started to wander out of the general proximity of the condo his parents had rented for their vacation. The building was nothing more than a solitary tower glued to the white sand next to the lagoon. That is how most of the area appeared; pockets of tropical forest mixed between sunset-hungry structures with obligatory pools, balconies, and patios. The exploration of the surrounding area was partially due to food.

Brandon had burned through all the provisions his parents had brought along. He was also bored, having exhausted the batteries for his Nintendo DS and laptop. He'd tried exploring a few units in the building, but he heard weight shifting around and a hissing sound behind the doors. A form even appeared in a window as he snuck along the side of the building. He couldn't look at it, but he knew it wasn't human. His skin felt like it was loose when he noticed it.

Instinct was telling him he was treading along the edge of a murderous abyss.

When Brandon finally journeyed further out, he was at least comforted to see that no one was immune from the rips of the shadow's claws. Gas stations, restaurants, offices, all buildings were shattered, scratched, and smeared over with thick ivy, which was illuminated in small dots of bright blue flowers. Brandon didn't enjoy exploring too much, because the silence of the crushed world would make him breathe quickly and his feet shake. When he first started walking down the gravel driveway of the condo towards Highway One, he would have to constantly stop and pee into the clusters of nearby palm trees. He'd never had a nervous bladder before, but the monsters had changed that too.

It was about a week ago, outside a now shattered Waffle House, that fortune decided to smile a little bit at Brandon.

Considering the circumstances, it was more of a grimace.

In front of the building, mixed in with some gnarly grass, concrete-sharp rubble, and blood-stained shoes and pants, was a long rifle with a scope. Brandon didn't know what type it was or anything. He just knew what it could do. He picked it up delicately. His dad had been a big Dungeons and Dragons player, and in one of the campaigns he'd played with Brandon his father was a marksman character. Brandon blinked a few tears apart with his eyes and shook his head.

"Wish you were here, dad," he said, lifting the weapon gently with his hands. A few vines snapped free of the stock and barrel.

The apocalypse didn't want to let it go.

Brandon tested placing the gun in his armpit, then shoulder, as more memories flooded back. Pizza, Sprite, paper plates, and dice with smears of cheesy oil.

"Initiative, roll for initiative," he said, through a cascade of tears.

Key Largo: 03

Juan counted the days at first, but it quickly became too hard. Ignorance was less of a sin and more of a survival tactic when living through an apocalypse. He knew it had been at least a few months since the night had woken to their drum, and the bladed shadows dripped out of every surface. It was like the world was nothing more than a haunted hourglass being turned upside-down. Juan knew that everyone was mostly dead back home in Mexico City if the monsters had appeared there as well. He had already decided that he'd never go back there to see his family. He just prayed to them at night before the drum started and that was all he could do.

Juan was lucky to be alive despite the depression, anxiety, hopelessness, PTSD, and paranoia that had appeared when civilization vanished. He was working on a shrimp boat just outside Key Largo. They were anchored on a lagoon, where the water was deep despite it being the Saltwater Everglades. If you fell into the shimmering blue, you could typically touch the sand-coral bottom. Juan didn't know how to swim very well, but the captain, an older man with a bald head and gray beard who'd been cut-in-half on the first night, told him in a grunting voice to just: "Stand up!"

There were two other fishermen on the boat when the devils appeared besides the captain. Both were killed instantly when the tall, pulsating shape crawled over the bow and wrapped each man in some sort of fabric. It pulverized both into bloody piles on the deck. Juan washed away their parts the next day with salt water. He hid the bucket he used. The sight of it made him nauseous.

Juan had been below decks when it happened. He hid inside a supply closet that was so disorganized it was like it had been destroyed already. Juan was short, stocky, with a full head of black hair and a square jaw. He made the rest of the crew look old, tired, and withered. Juan already felt unsafe aboard the ship before the nightmares had even arrived. The boat was called "The Clergy," and it was a two-level skiff with silver railings, a net on its back, and white paint flaking on the hull. He was surprised that the creatures simply missed him and moved on to attack other boats in the area.

Juan had survived for quite some time with the food that'd been packed on board. He collected rainwater to drink, and he also caught fish. He was too afraid to head towards shore with the boat, and too far away to try to swim. He didn't want to start the engine and have the creatures reappear. It was bad enough they turned the water over at night when their drum played. During the day, when the clouds were absent and the sun seared the water with lucidity, Juan could see black veins running throughout the sand. There were trickles of pulsing red light between each coil.

It was yet another reason he didn't want to leave the boat.

Those supernatural highways that now lived beneath the waves weren't as bad as the shadow that appeared when the drum would start. The moment that faraway boom would begin; a long, humanoid shape would glide beneath the boat towards the shore. It looked feminine. It had narrow legs, hips, and a tangle of hair, only it appeared more akin to tentacles that moved independently from its body. There was also a curve of folded fabric being dragged behind it. An unwilling child being dropped off at school. The water muted the color of the creature, but she still looked green and dark, like the plants that had consumed the earth in the wake of the drum. Juan was glad he couldn't see her face. Her back was always turned to him as she moved towards shore. This ignorance was the only gift he'd been given since it all began.

It was too soon to decide if being alive was a blessing or punishment in this eternal cataclysm.

It was nice to wake up at the same time every evening.

There were only a few days beneath the sapphire-silk waters of the tropics that she'd been interrupted. Once was when a manatee drifted over her pod. The shadow and shape of it made her think it was one of the human's ships. She could kill during the day if she wanted, but after smelling the water and separating the stench of the living through the salt and algae, she knew it was just another of the planet's non-toxic creatures.

It wasn't one that needed to be spoken to.

Another time she'd been woken was when a human child had glided over her in a rowboat. Whoever it was had not noticed the black shape in the water that she slept in. From above, it looked like a large disk with a sort of line through its center. Designs were etched across it like hieroglyphics. She didn't even know what they meant.

The vessel shuttered and shook. She could tell they were young and weak. She had a choice whether she could kill the little ones. With the adults, especially when the song was singing at night, it was harder, but she had free will. She wasn't as mindless as they thought. The way that little human paddled that boat made it look as if it were nothing, but a bug turned on its back.

How could she kill something that pitiful?

When the sound started, that ghostly echo from some faraway drum, her body would instantly stir. The door around her would open like an eyelid, and she'd be smelling in all directions for something to pulverize, mutilate, or eviscerate. When the song first started, she'd found hundreds of survivors each night to crush within the living fabric she carried on her back. Now, she seldom saw any, unless they became brave, stupid, or suicidal.

The audacity to be a hero was an easy arrogance to take advantage of in this apocalypse.

She knew the humans wouldn't be completely gone, no matter how many times they listened to the phantom song and carried out its slaughter. Her kind didn't know the world better than them, despite being older and wiser.

On her way to shore when the drum started, she'd pass a solitary vessel bowing on the waves. She could hear a human's heartbeat on it, but she could till he was scared and not a threat. Despite the commands of the voices in her head when the sound would start and the strange lust for human blood that would power the interactions between her cells, there were still moments of mercy in her mind. This man on the boat was one of them. She could tear it apart looking for him. She could even just puncture the hull with one of the tentacles in her hair by turning them into a tangled drill. She could let the man sink into the white sand.

She didn't do it.

Despite the voices in the song, the orders from the leaves curled together like mountains, it wasn't her purpose to kill every human.

She simply wanted to talk to them.

Juan didn't know what to do.

He rubbed his dry hands along his dark forehead and swayed his stocky frame back and forth. He wanted to jump in the water. It had been too long since he'd seen another human being, so when the young boy just ahead of him on shore stepped out of the cluster of palm trees shadowing the lagoon; it was almost a fantasy of sorts. The drum was sounding between the waves batting the hull. The twilight was bowing to the permanent gloom of night. The air smelled sweet with flowers, mixed with an aftertaste of salt from the orange-sunk water, which was temporarily echoing the glow of the ending sunset.

Juan still didn't know what to do.

The shape or the creature that had appeared with the drum had already swum beneath the vessel towards the boy, gliding effortlessly. A fleshy current broke free from the deep. It did this every evening when the demonic metronome played. The monster's appearance was as consistent as the sun setting and rising. It would arrive on land and stalk for survivors. The boy was in the open, and even from the faraway distance of his anchored ship, Juan could tell the monster would be on top of him in moments.

Juan knew what to do.

He ran into the pilot's house just above the bow of the ship where he'd been watching. He quickly tried to start the engine, but the key clicked back at him in empty aches. He had hoped he could start the boat and maybe get the boy's attention on the lagoon, so he'd see her approaching. Too much complacency at the beginning of this apocalypse was now taking a toll. Juan had always secretly wanted to start the boat and run away, but he didn't. He didn't know about where she might be during the day. How she might be woken up and try to wrap her tentacles around the boat. Now, when he needed the engine to run, it was as empty as the sky.

Juan quickly dug through the cabinets beneath the wheel and tore out the emergency kit. It beamed red in the clutter. Inside was a flare gun with one shot. He held the gun and sighed. He was saving it to be rescued, but nobody was coming except for the monsters. He ran out of the bridge and down to the railing facing the strip of beach. She was almost to the shore. The boy was still standing by the woods, blissfully unaware of the incoming abomination. The air was salty and quiet to the drum. How could he not know to hide right now? If he survived this long surely, he knew what the sound summoned.

Dusk was fading away. In just a few minutes the beach would be nothing more than a faded line atop the bowing waves. Juan aimed the flare into the sky just above where the boy had been. He closed his eyes, thought of his family and friends, hoped he would meet them on the other side and pulled the trigger. There was a burst of air pressure, a snarl of sparks, and the arc of the flare gliding upwards over the water. The monster instantly broke the surface in a violent spray, twisting back at the boat with her eyeless face. She'd been betrayed. Juan dropped the gun and sunk back into the boat.

He knew he'd be dead soon.

Brandon couldn't discern the shape coming towards him from the shore. The darkness of night had hit so quickly with the drum, it was almost cartoonish how swiftly the daylight had fled. He didn't know if the creature noticed him from the beach. It was tall, almost ten feet, with a stretched body of tendrils, limbs, and fabric. Attached to its back was a long coil of blue light, which snaked out into the shallows. A road into a glimmering, sunken city.

Brandon felt hypnotized by their glow. The phantom trails singing some song to the curiosity behind his eyes.

The lagoon stunk of salt. It mixed with the sweetness of the flowers, which had sprouted up with the apocalypse and drum. Even in the remnants of the day, the smell of those pastel bits of flora still haunted Brandon wherever he went. The air was slightly cool, enough to make Brandon feel cold, even though he was sweating profusely as he watched the monster. The hanging tentacles around her hidden head looked moved independently in snarls and hisses. They had their own intentions on what to hunt tonight.

Brandon held the rifle tight to his shoulder and knelt into the bushes just below the swaying palm trees. For a second, he looked through the red scope with his right eye. He'd dropped the gun a few days early dodging one of the living shadows behind a Starbucks. The lens was shattered. He was too nervous to remember that'd happened. This made him feel stupid and underprepared.

The monsters had that effect on you, especially the kind that lived in the water.

Brandon could've focused on the bladed shadows stalking the condominium where his parents were vacationing when they were killed, or the big one at the shipyard off the highway, which had a claw so massive a trench in the ground trailed behind wherever it wandered. For some reason, this ocean devil that appeared along this white beach at night was what he wanted to spend his few bullets on. He'd practiced firing the gun just off the road where he hid inside the condo. He wanted a place to run and hide if they appeared. During the day they were rare, but at night they seemed to occupy every corner and streetlight.

Brandon took a shallow breath and licked his lips. He had been aiming the gun at her monstrous shape for so long he felt as if she could see him and was daring him to fire.

So, he did.

The sound and blast seemed stronger at night than when he practiced beneath the sun. The nozzle coughed out a bubble of fire that crackled sideways. The plants around him startled to the side. His hands shook to the vibration and his shoulder pinched. He'd gotten used to firing it, but the stress of being so close to one of them had made his muscles tighten up like a stale rope. Brandon fired each shot until the chamber clicked empty and a small trail of sulfur smoke crossed his face.

None of the shots had worked against her. If Brandon could even see in the darkness, he would have watched her mushroom-topped shield attached to her back, absorb each bullet into this leathery wall.

A flare suddenly burst off the shore. There was a boat sitting in the lagoon. Brandon hadn't noticed it. The chemical illumination sizzled the dark. For one simple second, she looked back at the boat.

Then, she charged at him with a hiss that drowned out that distant beat of the drum. Her shape was massive and flowing. It was almost like the night was parting to avoid her. Brandon immediately regretted his bravery, boldness, and brashness. He lamented his anger, curiosity, and ambition. Now, all he could do was run and hide.

That was the only thing that would keep him alive.

Tonight, it would not.

Beware the Ills

The Three Clawed Man

I see it.

It is just ahead of me. We've been on the sea for weeks. It's an ugly trip. The water is inky and violent, to the point that the sun doesn't even want to fall on it. Maybe it thinks it's contagious. Maybe it thinks it's poisonous. This Cursed Island. This island of nightmares. Whatever it is. Whatever the sun might think, I'm at the island now. I can see it.

And I'm not impressed.

For some monster maker, some abomination spawner, and some legendary killer, it really is just a line of trees, lumps of rock by black water, and an empty beach. The only semblance of civilization is a leftover ship from the previous failed invasion idling on the waves like a half-gutted fish. It's just an island. A cursed one, but an island. The people will bleed the same way. The guardian will too. Its magic is fixed. Kain told me all about it. I listened. I'm ready.

I did not want to land with the rest of the invasion. I'm attached to a balloon of sorts, with some steam engines on its back in a mechanical cube. The engineers explained to me how it worked. They're funny little people with fuzzy eyebrows, curled backs, and pimply ears. They were nervous when talking to me. All sweaty, edgy, and mumbled. I make most people like that. At first it annoyed me when father let me out into the world for various hires. Now, I like it. No idle conversation. Just start, then finish. Hunt, then kill.

They offered me a boat, but even I'm not foolish enough to tempt the Wrappers down in the depths. We've known species like them before. Big, gangly things that drip with tentacles and hooks. We eat their smaller sisters and brothers. I've seen them grilled in the cities by the coast. I don't eat seafood. I can always taste the sea. I don't need that distraction when I'm trying to enjoy my meal. Eating with a claw on your right forearm is difficult enough. 20 years removed from having it grafted and I still find it awkward. Father wasn't wrong when he said it would change my life. I didn't think he would be wrong. That is not his tendency.

This is the final hunt, the ending mission, the bloody apex of the mountain top. After I finish off their new Guardian, steal the Leftovers, and claw down any resistance, well, it is over. I can return to the Empty Plains, and have this cursed extra claw clipped off my wrist.

When I told them the hand to put it on, I lied, knowing they wouldn't listen to me. I told them I was right-handed. Father didn't know which hand was dominant. I was hurt that he didn't know. I told him before. I wouldn't tell him again. He didn't pay attention to me in the right way. If it was the scratch, stab, or slash of my claw, he would remember every iota of physics to my technique.

Father chose what he thought was my dominant hand to put the blade. The Flesh Smith didn't care where he put the claw. He just listened to father. He pointed behind my wrist. Made a little circle with his massive finger, and then patted on my skin with his typical, small smile. It was the type of smirk that didn't really commit to an emotion, but more a social norm. The type you would make to demonstrate how to act appropriately, but not authentically so.

It was a gesture of an animal trying to be human.

The monsters in the waves know I've been talking to them. I'm more than a hundred feet above the water, which thrashes, twists, and turns against the beachhead. It's loud. Enough to rumble over the contraption I've let carry me like a baby bird over the violent surf. They still know I'm here. They're floating upwards. They're great rubbery skeletons, stretched and swaying in the depths. The ripples and froth mute their hideousness, not that I would mind. Enough time hunting and killing in this ugly world of ours gives you a somewhat ironic affinity for the monstrous. I would like to pretend I'm much different than the demons floating beneath my feet.

I'm not really, I just have more style.

They're going to surface. They must be hungry. What leviathans must they hunt down in the dark? What must hunt them? Everyone is another part of another's food chain. They're almost here. Their white glow fills in the black. They look like ghosts rising. They could be fluid smoke, only they're coming together. They strike upwards. The froth spouts and splits. I bend my left wrist on the cold handle mounted to the engine of my balloon. It rises just enough for their tangle of tentacles to writhe against the empty air beneath my boots. The thunder of their movement is fantastic. The surface splits against their hunger. It is so natural and beautiful, I wish I could do the same without hesitation, but even I have my limits to carnage. Father knew this, like all famous hunters from our house. He knew it. No women. No children. Just men. We're the source of the strife anyways. We've stacked the world in our favor. It makes sense to always have an executioner ready to cull our ugly herd. I'm trained to be an ax, block, and noose.

They try again, again, and again below me. How do they see me? Again, I'm flabbergasted by their one eye. It's a snow-white disk. It must be an endless tunnel between the two worlds. Water, air, then back again. How nice it must be to be born a killer and not forged into one. I never thought I'd get jealous of a squid.

They flick and flutter. Little children pawing for candy at the confectioner. I was never able to do it. I was paraded past that colorful shop with the blue ribbons on its door by my father's right hand. He kept it tightly gripped on my shoulder. I even saved a little bit of money for it when I could wander by myself. Not that I would ever have to pay. All the shops in the nearby city of Pendulum would never require me to pay for anything. Our hunting house, our emblem, never bought anything because we could kill anything. You don't deny the killers their bread and milk. Still, I wanted to be normal. I wanted to pay for that candy. It is still hidden away in my childhood home, snuck away in a ceramic clock by my bed. Maybe someday soon, after this last job, I'll spend it.

This is the last one.

They're still flailing. I'm amazed. What stamina beasts have, even the underwater ones. I know my father would want me to be like them. I know it. He would have me turned into one if he could. I'm not truly enhanced like Kain's creations. He sent two of them here already. Where are they now? The Guardian cut them down. You can't beat the original. You can't beat years of training in the Empty Plains.

I'm past them now. They've given up. They didn't have to try that long to figure I was out of their reach. Their hunger made them. It dictates. It commands. How their bellies must growl in the deep. Do they guard these shores because they know what sleeps in the Diamond Town? Are they aware of the sleeping devil cuddled amongst the pine trees and snow bluffs? I would assume. Animals are wise to a world our senses can't feel. They map out all their invisible trails, and sniff along them, leaving us humans in their hidden wake. I'm okay being left behind. I don't want to be on every trail. I don't want to know everything.

I just want to finish on this island, then retire to the plains. The claws. My armor. They all want it. The skin that grows up and around my third claw, wants it to end the most. How confused my flesh is. I feel bad about it. I tell it not to grow there. I tell it every morning, day, and night. Father said old hunters from our house had inhuman discipline. They could control their organs, blood, and flesh at the most micro of levels. Some of them had extensions like me. Some, not all. He said they controlled their body around these blades and points.

My father is a liar.

I'm over the beach now. That is far enough. I let go of the infant of a flying machine and fall through the air. I aim for a thicker snowbank, just up the shore. There were traps set further into the woods. I doubt the new Guardian has had time to rearm them. They're probably still wondering about the voices and figures. The woods won't spare them that. It won't. This Cursed Island has its own gravity. They're pulled by it. I am not. This is not my home. This is not my land.

The open air always wakes me up. Not being attached to the ground or the sky, you feel free, alive, and untethered to all the ugliness that my reality has to offer. I wonder often about the other reality, the ones that live their lives in such blissful subservience to mundane duties. Farm, harvest, build, sell, paint, draw, and all the working world outside of the Empty

Plains. They don't know the splits of skin beneath your toes while outrunning a troll in the petrified wood. They don't know the begging and screaming the target makes when my claws are finally free. They're lucky. I won't know it soon either. The Guardian doesn't have that option. The devil sleeping on this island demands it.

The phantom stipulation is unrelenting.

I land on the snow, ice, and dirt. Nothing. No magic spells. No cloud of poison. No possessed townsfolk sprinting at me from the quiet needle trees and their towering stumps. Just a quiet forest. A turning beach of black water. A landscape of white humps of mixed snow. I take a deep breath. I check my cloak and claws. My beige fabric hangs down on my back and front in a baggy triangle. It doesn't cover my knees or black boots. There are bits of silver beads sewn into the material, to catch sunlight or torchlight in combat and disorient my attackers or defenders. The cloak was webbed of dust phoenix feathers and night wolf fur. Both creatures can resist arrowheads and sword strikes. Our family killed them. Another treasure of the natural world put upon the altar of my ancestry. Such sacrifices are legion.

I run.

Trees. Hills. Incomplete paths. Divots of uneven snow and earth. They all flash, rise, drop, and spread out before me in a quiet, snowy elegance. There is no wildlife. No real sound except the wind battering by me. Occasionally the white beads along the dreadlocks of my brown hair clatter together. Not a fashion choice by me. Another fighting tactic. Longer hair hides my emotions, movements, and disorients onlookers, violent or peaceful. My face is nothing special anyways. White, weathered, quiet, like these hills. My eyes are dark, my forehead, cheeks, and nose scarred from skirmishes. My teeth are clean and straight. Father made sure they were straightened, cleaned, and polished. There is a political element to my job, a language beyond my claws. I don't like it, but it's there. I cannot be too battle worn. I need to be able to appear and communicate.

I don't like it.

Still nothing but a snowy island with an empty forest. I know to head north, towards the legendary Diamond Town. I know the layout, the broken walls they call the Shingles, and the famous city in the clearing at the foot of the mountains. Do the citizens know? Do they have any idea about what sleeps in their city? I'm sure they don't. This island wouldn't be what it is if they knew. Their footsteps trod on a devil's face. Their shadows are its breath. Their homes are just bumps along its demonic spine.

They have no clue.

I keep running. Someone is following me. I can hear echoing through the solemn trunks and branches. The snow muffles it, but I'm trained to listen, to watch my shadows like they watch me. They're getting closer. They're fast. They could be an Ill, but they wouldn't attack by themselves. They work in teams and clusters. Our recon made that clear. They rely on numbers because of their weaponry and armor. The figure is ahead of me. They flanked me. I'm impressed. I know who it is. They're masked in trees and snow, crouched, and carrying something long and obscene. I stop and casually bend down. I ready my chain claw beneath my billowing cloak. It's on a long black chain. It has five curved points and two slashing round edges. I can hit them from here. I can take down the trees if I must and use the falling snow to disorient them.

"I thought you were dead?" I asked the shadow.

"I should be," they answer back. It's her. I can remember her voice. Another of Kain's gifts to this world. She hasn't had her Blood Fire in a while. I assume she ran out. How can she be alive?

"The Guardian didn't kill you? That's odd," I ask.

"It is," she replies.

"Why don't you come out of the shadows. I'm not here for you. We represent the same shield."

I hear her shuffle slightly.

"Have they appointed a new Guardian yet on the walls?" I ask slowly, walking to my right. I still can't see her. Why would she be hiding? I trained with her before the invasions launched.

"Yes," she replies.

"So, our timing was in vain. A week equals ten years in combat time. Where's your lover? Any other survivors?"

"He's dead. They're all dead," she whispers.

"The new or old Guardian killed him?"

"The old."

"Who killed that one? You?" I inch closer in a crouch.

She hesitates. I hear metal and skin shift. They twinkle and ache against the quiet snow. She could be making a combat posture.

"A mistake," she whispers.

"The cannibal?"

"Yes."

"That's a twist."

"It was poison. The cannibal proved to be more powerful than we thought."

She pauses again.

"Or the Guardian had given up," she whispers.

"Are you coming back beneath the shield then? The second wave is here. They'll be landing within hours."

She must be weak from exposure, lack of food and water, and the echoes of war. She might be enhanced by that mad scientist, Kain, but a week in this perpetual winter would slow anyone down.

"No," she replied.

"Are you wounded? It can't have been easy out here alone?"

She is silent.

"Have they brought him and his son?" She whispers.

I wait.

"Are you talking about Kain? Yes. He is here."

"And his son?"

I squinted looking for an answer. The cold numbs my eyelids. A few flakes of snow buzzed by my eyelashes.

"He does not have his children."

"He called me his daughter."

I nod, but I do not know if she can see me.

"The Living Shadow."

"Yes."

I sigh.

"He's here as well."

"Where?"

"On a boat with Kain. He wouldn't be anywhere else."

"Why did they bring him?"

The breeze kicks the branches around. Snow swirls up and down.

"Because you failed, Berserker."

"I stopped fighting."

"Why?"

"The Guardian spared me. He spared the Ills. He wasn't listening to his blood song. He died correcting the mistake."

I can't hide my eyebrows rising with surprise.

"I see, but the new Guardian?"

"She hasn't left the city, yet."

"I'm surprised."

"Don't be. Something is happening to this city, Slaver. Something is happening to this curse, beyond the body. Beyond what is hidden beneath the mortar, dirt, and frost."

I pause. It has been so long since someone has called me by my name. Everyone just calls me the Three Clawed Man.

"That's interesting."

I relax my pose. There is no violence here. She wouldn't bother with this information if she wanted me dead. This is an honest conversation. I didn't expect such a confrontation when I immediately landed on the Cursed Island. She must have been waiting in the eves on the shoreline for the next wave. She knew it was coming. Whose side is she on now? The silence, the bristling trees, and the snowy wind seem to be curious as well.

"So, what do you want?" I finally ask.

"I don't know," she replies. "And you?"

"I'm going to kill the Ancients, take their pieces back to Kain, and leave this island to grow as it should have centuries ago."

"Kain cannot have the bones. He'll make more monsters. Just like me. Just like the Living Shadow. I have none of the fallen inside of me. Who knows how my brother will react to being on this soil, where the demon fell to earth."

I tightened my grip on my claw.

"I don't care who ends up with the bones. I don't. The Empty Plains do not care either. I just want what is mine."

"And what is yours?"

As her words end, I can see her tighten up slowly. She was smart to mask herself beneath the tree. The shadows are just right. I don't know where to aim.

"The ending. This is my ending. The last job for my house. I capture those bones, and our contract with the Plains is complete. No more claws. No more killing. Just a farmhouse, the woods, and my dogs. Nothing here or there."

"The Guardian had a pet. We killed it."

Again, I'm surprised.

"Really? I thought they worked alone."

"Not this one."

"Well, you said he was different."

I strike. My claw is out in a glimmer of fanned points and black metal through the white air. Its five blades are iron fingers. Its palm and sides curled blades for slashing and cutting. I use it to wound. It whistles. An instrument only capable of a requiem. It is beautiful. How can she react? How can she dodge? I aim low for one of her legs. I just need to wound her to bring her back to her Kain. It'll be one less obstacle. The claw splits the branches of curtained green and needle. It cuts and crunches them simultaneously in a snap.

The natural world is always an innocent bystander to our violent machinations.

My claw strikes something solid and metallic. It pings on the winter air in a metallic echo. I twist, pulling the weapon backwards. She was ready. I turn my torso, using the momentum to carry my claw to me. Something parts the remaining tree branches. It's a spear. Her lover's spear. I remember from the briefing and training. I duck below it. It was too heavy, and I'm too far away for it to collide. She knew it was faulty. She knew I was too quick. She didn't want to hurt or kill me.

I blink three times.

I know the berserker is gone. It was smart. Very smart. The dialogue surprised me. I had lowered my guard.

"You are slower than I thought, the island won't let you live long at that speed," she yells from somewhere around me. She knows that I don't have the time to hunt her. Once the invasion lands the Ancients and their forces will be on guard. Now is my chance to sneak into the city.

"I didn't want you dead. I just wanted you out of the picture so I could focus," I yell back to the quiet trees.

"Don't underestimate this island. I know you're famous. I know. But like I told you before, something is happening here beyond the curse, beyond the Plains, and beyond everything."

Her voice whistles away in the snow and wind.

"That is so needlessly cryptic," I howl over the invisible din.

Silence, she must really be gone. I'm impressed by her stealth. She wasn't like this before. She was a cleaver, a walking and glowing porcelain statue of unfettered bloodlust. She's right. Something is happening here.

I run.

More trees. More hills. More clearings with the occasional ice-free stream crossing through. I'm memorizing the smells. Soil, pine, frost, and ice. It is a sterile mixture, with extraordinarily little heat or warmth. It almost stinks like it isn't alive. A frozen corpse on the mortician's table. Smell is part of my training. You can sense things before they physically approach. Father loved to train and develop that skill. He said he'd sew a dead dog's nose to my face if he could. He always hated animals. He was jealous of them. They had no assassins' house to uphold. No credo. No pledge. No shield.

Simplicity should always be admired and never condemned.

The more complexity we discover in our world, whether it is for science or war or self, you begin to understand just how complicatedly beautiful our existence truly is. So, when a basic harmony fulfills itself, you can only admire how it maintains its own sense of purpose. I doubt people know these thoughts when they see me or fall beneath my claws.

I've hit a large clearing that splits into a valley. It's filled with uneven clusters of trees. The snow reflects the muted brightness from the clouds, making the ground look brighter. This must be it. This must be the famous graveyard. The river will be behind it. The battle there slowed everything down. They never would have had to cross it if the airship hadn't failed. Nobody could have imagined the Guardian being capable of taking down an airship, but he did. The previous guardians had always won, but the Plains thought this was our best chance considering our use of the steam engine. Still, we were thwarted. This Guardian was special. I believe the berserker.

I would have liked to meet him.

At first there were just shapes looking out from between the trees and branches in broken postures. Then, from between the beams and their barky, velvet tendrils were piles of shields, swords, arrows, axes, spears, knives, pikes, and even a few claws. They were also stuck in various tree trunks. It went out for rows and rows of trees. Then came the machines, a whole buffet of twisted metal and rusted engines standing, sitting, laying, leaning, and hanging upon one another. They were spread out. They were dense. They were covered in frost. Some were clean and had just been dragged there. Others looked before the Plains. I know this island, this cursed jewel, has been on the horizon for many kingdoms and governments throughout the endless corridors of time and space. Many know its secrets. It wasn't until Kain came along that they could be harnessed and used. It wasn't until the airships and steam engines. Now we're not just on the doorstep of the Cursed Island. We're kicking it in with machines and monsters.

The graveyard is endless. I keep thinking I'm through it or on the outskirts. There are more and more. I can see why this place is legendary. I can see why this place is a myth. The air feels dead, but also alive around all this rust and bone. There are bodies. Some are new, from within the week of our first invasions. Others are just skeletons. Macabre keepsakes of long-lost expeditions and missions. There are piles upon piles. The trees, the snow, the frost, and all the many decorations of the natural world do their best to obscure the leftover gore, but it is not enough. I'm climbing mountains of the dead. They're thick under foot.

How did they know what this place was? All these white skulls and empty eyes. Could they dream, when they still could, of what this island is to the greater world? I feel bad for them. I know there were no real answers for the grunts and peons of this conquest. If we're successful, maybe their souls will be a little bit more still.

I can feel their undead curiosity.

Still no end to them; the always frozen dead. My boots have small claws in their soles and sides to run slicker in snow. They have hidden blades too, for kicking and stabbing, but I've never used them before. They aren't a real tool in my violent repertoire. Everything has given me an edge, both with skill and physically.

After all my missions and killing, even I cannot ignore the aura of this island. The perpetual white sky, falling snow, and quiet trees. The crunching of frost beneath my sprints. It has all the air of the otherworldly.

This is a good job to end on.

I'm happy to be here.

Leave the Name

They picked me.

I didn't think they would. I'm older. I have children. My husband died in the assault on the city. They dragged his body out from beneath a broken wall. His arms were gone. The blood had frozen to the bricks. I didn't feel anything. Maybe that's the sword. They said it would change me. They said I would change not immediately, but with each passing second. What's the difference? He was a worthless man. A drunk who knew the stained windows of the pub more than his son's faces. He was either always sad, or always angry. There was nothing in-between. Always rotating between hot and cold, fire and ice.

I wanted to believe him when he said he could change. I wanted to. Each time, he'd make a little progress, then slide backwards down the bottom of the ale glass. He lived there. It was the only thing he ever cared about. They burnt his body with all the others who died in the battle. The outlanders pierced the Shingles and nearly sacked the city. The Guardian appeared just moments before we were all cleaved to bits. The Ills helped as well. They saved us. They're our allies now. I still don't trust them. They're everywhere. I didn't know the mountains had so many.

Before they picked me, or the sword did, I didn't know anything it seemed like. Nobody wanted me to know how to protect this city. Nobody. Now, I will know everything.

Or so they tell me.

After the ritual on the shingles with the Ancients, they gave me the sword. They put adults and children together when they dropped the coal. They would have you hold the sword, and a flaming rock. On the stone there were letters, the old script from the times before our common language. If you could hold both items for more than a few seconds without flinching, you were it. I did that. I held it longer. I could not feel the fire. I mean I could, but it was only pain. I felt power too. I felt in control. I wanted to be the Guardian. I didn't want to be a shadow dragging her husband out of the pub anymore.

So, here I am.

They gave me armor. It's black, plated, with a single shoulder piece that is curved outwards in a blade. The Ancients said the previous Guardian used it as a weapon. I can't picture that behavior. They told me not to think about it. The sword would tell me. All I had to do was listen. It has its own bloodlust inertia. They had the armor bent and fitted to my tall, slender shape. I'm pale, blue-eyed, with long black hair that curls past my shoulders. I'm plain. Nothing special. Another laborer in the city, living from coin to coin.

Now, I have the sword.

When they handed it to me, I could hear voices. They were brief. Whispers. A faint wind of them. They brushed against my ears but no one else noticed. The Ancients said it. They said the sword has a life of its own. The blade will adjust to its new wielder, whether I'm ready or not to use it. They said to relax. How can I relax? They're back at the Shingles. They're protected. Some survivors have taken the armor and weapons of the dead soldiers and formed a small army. The Ills are there too, guarding the many walls. Easy for those old men to have the young to fight. Easy for them to be positive.

They're not where I am.

I'm supposed to meet the Ills near the shore for a counterattack. They're going to land on the beach and we're going to attack. We're not hoping to win. Just slow them down. Maybe lure the ghosts in the deep upwards for them to wrap their ships. It is their prince's idea. He is the leader. I don't trust him. They saved us, but I can't stomach it. I'm fighting three decades of hatred, bred, and bottled by our small city. I hate the Ancients and elders for all their resistance to change. The sword reminds us that force and violence is absolute.

When they handed me the weapon, it was straight, long, with a standard cross hilt. It was black on the grip. It was silver on the blade. It had two edges and a needle point. They said it may change shape. They said it might not. They are old. Their voices crack and struggle. I could barely understand them. Their words are not used often. I had never spoken to the ancients before. We were on the Shingles when we spoke, shortly after they fitted me for the armor. They gave me a red cloak too. It is bright, livid, a crimson star amongst all the gray, white, and black of this snowy island. It is like theirs, the Ancients, but tighter, and not as lumpy.

I don't want to look like them, but I do.

Maybe that was the idea. I'm elite. I'm special. They gave me the sword. They want me to understand this connection. I don't care about being special. I do feel a difference in my posture and my breath. Both feel effortless and unattached. Someone else was holding me up.

The Ancients said they would watch my children. They would be in one of the keeps during the next assault. I didn't want to leave them. I have two sons. They're six and eight. Both are pale, brown-eyed, and curly haired. Roth and Gale. Roth is the older one. Gale the younger. I named them after heroes from the stories. I wanted them to

65

have real lives. To live real dreams across the city, as limited as they are. We're confined. Trapped almost. I can't give them much to dream about, but I didn't build the city here. Only the ancients know who did.

The here and now. The here and now. They kept saying that. They kept telling me to focus on what was around me. The sword will help. It was made to help. I can't fall back on memories, family, the life before the burn marks on my hand and the smell of my burning skin. They said the past will distract me. I'll need a singular vision, unclouded by trauma and time. How is that possible? How can I forget the pain of where I came from in just a day or two? The Ancients assured me that I would. Many, many words. They never spoke to me before.

I was nobody.

That thought won't leave me. No matter how many hills I run up and down. No matter how many trees I weave between. No matter how many times I skip, jump, and roll between white rocks with green moss caked around their bottoms. The sword is giving me speed already. My body doesn't ache or feel cold. I sprint and dash endlessly. My lungs quicken, but don't stop. They said this would happen, but again I'm nobody.

I stopped when I reached a river.

There were whispers. They were both everywhere and nowhere. Snow was falling. It was quiet besides the wind and the bits of ice bouncing into one another on the partially frozen water. The blackness of that flowing liquid fills me with dread. I never learned how to swim. No one taught me. No one cared. Did the previous Guardian know how? Did his predecessors? Did somebody teach them? I wish I could concentrate on the world around me. War is waiting on the forest's edge. Death, dismemberment, the blood of outlanders, Ills, and villagers will run together into one ruby ocean. From the siege, when the outlanders broke our walls, I watched the Guardian fight the blond demon with blue fire. They fought like poetry, weaving, waxing, twisting through one another in violence. Before I got the sword, before I knew my husband was dead, before all of it, I liked the sight of it.

Keep running. Just keep running.

I hop from shard to shard of white ice drifting across the river. We call this river the Bends. I think it is the Bends. I know the names of our city and its outskirts, but I never really left them. Maybe that is why I hesitate. I've never had to put the names into practice. My name is Catrina. Yes, Catrina. I don't know why there is hesitation with that as well. It is just my name. There is nothing more attached to it. I don't know why it sinks me. Maybe it's the wind? The howl of air hitting me from all directions. In the city the walls, alleys, boulevards, and buildings take that brunt, that force, that gale. The forest doesn't care enough to stop it. The trees have their own heartbeat. I can almost hear them. Maybe it is because I'm out here for the first time. Maybe that is my own heartbeat?

Is there a difference?

I stop after I cross the Bends. I don't even remember jumping across it fully. My mind is here and everywhere, all at once. I need to be patient with myself. Yesterday, I was still helping other citizens crawl out of the rubble. Many are still missing. With the cold and lack of food, they're probably dead. They might be better off with what's arriving. The Ancients said that this could be the worst invasion yet, and they've seen a maelstrom of them over the centuries. How do they live so long? What is their secret? Why would they want to live so long on such a dull, emotionless island? Have they not grown tired of the same city, same walls, and same gray mountains lining the horizon? I am. Now that I'm outside the Shingles I can see how trapped I was. There are a million different things to see, hear, and smell.

I'm into the woods fully. My speed is picking up. I can almost feel myself watching myself, as if I were standing outside of my own body as it's moving. I almost feel like one of those wooden puppets on a string, the ones theaters use during festivals inside the city. I feel detached, but in control. The sensation feels both troubling, and natural. I want to stop and think about it more, but my legs just keep turning. I jump, twist, step, sprint, and lunge between trees. The sword on my back started heavy, awkward, and clumsy. The more I move, the closer to it I feel, as if it were weightless, or an extension of my physical body. I must stop ruminating. I need to focus on the here and now.

I stop.

For the simplest of seconds between the flurries, clouds, and winds, I heard a voice echo out at me from the stumps, needles, and snowy rocks. The needle trees grow in abundance beyond the Shingles. Their dark green has a glow to it, as if they were aflame to some hidden, verdant energy in their frost-covered roots. They're probably just reflecting the snow-light.

"Hello?" I yell out. My hand goes for the hilt of the sword behind my shoulder without hesitation. Before my greeting can echo, it is in my hand and dangling downward. My forearm flexes along with my wrist, but I can hold it. The sword feels lighter. It is lighter. It is curved. It was straight before.

"Hello?" I yell again. I crouch down slightly.

There is laughter bouncing out from the empty spots between the trees and snowflakes. It rises and falls all around me, sticking to

67

the flurries. My skin snaps to it. My shoulders tremble. I don't know why someone would be laughing. I wouldn't understand why. This is war. The Ills are positioning themselves on the shore for the next invasion force. Nobody is outside the Shingles except for me and the Ills, plus a few citizens who have formed a ragtag militia of sorts with the previous invader's weapons. None of them will speak or interfere with me. The Ancients were clear about that before we broke apart for the counterattack. The Ills, except for their prince and his bodyguards, refuse to look at me. So down the townspeople. I feel powerful, but still invisible.

I continue to run.

Again, the voice sounds. This time louder, almost concrete, and clear amongst the eves. I study the white air, the cloudy sky, and the layers of spiked greenery. My skin tenses again. I'm looking in every direction. I want to know who would speak to me. Who could it be? Who would be out here? A straggler? A lost Ill? Who could it be? I want to see them. I can barely handle the sword. I can't have phantoms torturing me this early in the campaign.

"I see, so you can hear, but can't see me. What a conundrum. I didn't think this experience would be easy, but this is certainly frustrating," a voice said. It was low, male, and jarring amongst the whirling winter light.

"Who? Where are you?" I whispered, spinning in an endless circle.

"You can stop moving. I'm not anywhere near you. I'm someplace. A corridor. A dark corridor. With mist and walls, but I can see you through it. It's thinning. All of it is thinning. I'm wondering if I'll be able to. If I'll be able to move out of here."

"I don't understand, you're speaking to me, but you're not here?"

I was starting to feel crazy. Was this part of the sword?

"I'm not with you, but I'm behind you in a room. I'm watching you. It is hard to describe beyond that. I'm not alone, there are others too."

I'm getting cold. I hadn't really noticed it until now. Maybe pausing. Maybe focusing on the voice. Something about the tone. It feels familiar. It feels like home, like a layer of warmth around the hearth you always know is there. Our home in the city was run-down. We were poor. We all knew how the warmth cracked through the bricks around our fireplace.

We had memorized them.

"I don't want you to slow down. I'm not important. I'm dead, after all. I died on the shore. Haukter killed me. He took everything I had to kill him. Everything. Every little bit of me, both from the sword

68

and my body. I shattered it. Broke the blade. That was my opening. It had a million hides. I could not hurt him. Not that I wanted to," the voice said. It was over my shoulder. It felt next to me. It was clear. It was there.

"You, you were the Guardian?" I whispered.

"You'll have to speak louder, where I am, there is an awful lot of mumbling and shuffling happening."

"You are the Guardian?"

"I was the Guardian, as I had said, and you shouldn't make me repeat myself, especially about something so personal, but I'm dead. Haukter poisoned. We fought in the graveyard. We fought hard. It was the greatest battle I could ever hope for. Complete violence. An apex of slashes, dodges, and strikes. We altered the landscape. We left the ground and trees still talking about it today."

I tried to think about what was happening. I had just been picked. I had just been fitted for my armor. Now, a phantom was on my back, whispering of old battles and deaths just days ago.

"I know you might be in disbelief, but you'd be served to abandon that mindset. You have a living sword sitting on your back, you'd better start thinking that you're more myth than reality."

I could hear a slight sigh in the ghoulish echo.

"I wish I had figured that out sooner in my handling of the sword."

A silence of snowfall took hold.

"This is odd," I said to myself.

"It is," he replied. "But again, having judgment towards what is real isn't necessary nor helpful. You're an adult. I was a child when the sword started speaking to me. That reality was all I knew. I remember nothing before it. Those memories continued to shatter and shatter, till they were just dust."

Another deep breath and pause from this hidden voice.

"There are more invaders. The Ancients panicked after my killing and picked an adult. I'm guessing the pale men in metal shells weren't just one invasion. It didn't seem like a single incursion. They had the technology to launch many. Airships. Boats. Walking machines with gears for guts. The whole thing did not seem limited. Violence has an endless array of creativity to power it."

I'm thinking of questions. Many of them. I don't know where to ask them.

"So, you're not dead, but you're somewhere else?" I finally said. It was easier to speak than wrangle these racing thoughts.

"I appear to be dead. I know Haukter killed me. I'm just not where I'm supposed to be. There are others with me, or what used to be others. They're dried out. Husks just piled along the walls. Men

69

and women. They've got armor, cloaks, and the thread sewn across their eyes and lips."

More breath and sighs.

"They're not the best company," he laughs.

"I wouldn't imagine so," I reply. "Who are they?"

"I appreciate that you think I know these things. I do. But the questions are getting intrusive. Do I need to remind you that I, in fact, died?"

"I thought you told me to suspend my disbelief. To give myself up to the magic of the sword?" I snort.

"I did, but don't suspend your sense of logic. That can still operate in disbelief. Everyone in that cold, brick of a town has that fog on them. The Ancients have thoroughly polluted your minds. The sword you're carrying cuts through the naivety. At least you'll start to see with real eyes soon enough."

"Statements like that just want me to ask more questions," I said.

Another sigh. They nearly match the questions in quantity.

"This is a lousy purgatory."

I stop myself. I've been walking. When did I start walking? When did it happen? I'm out of the river valley, and into some of the thicker parts of the forest. The trees are blotting out the white sky. The air has shadows that feel like people, as if they're standing over me. I'm surrounded, but there is no one there. I'm alone. Except for the voice.

"What? Didn't I need to tell you that too? Didn't I? You might move and act without being conscious of it. I know that's hard to explain and understand. Believe me, I don't have that answer. I am just familiar with the question. The sword is both asking it and withholding the answer. It has gravity. You're just being pulled along."

There was another pause.

"Just like me."

Something rattled behind. There was a hiss and gasp of sorts, the type an animal makes when being harnessed or dragged away. My shoulders felt lighter. My arms were no longer heavy. My thoughts were my own. There wasn't an echo. It was gone. I knew it wasn't there anymore.

"Are you there?" I asked.

Just silence. My heartbeat. Bending eves. Snowflakes glancing at my shoulders, armor, and hair.

"I said, are you there?" I asked again.

Nothing. No animosity. No quick retort. No undead cleverness ready to tell me how to survive. Not that he did a fantastic job of it. I wouldn't be here with the sword strapped to my back if he hadn't failed. I'm here because he failed.

"Okay, I'm going to stop talking to myself?"

A final silence.

I take more notice of my surroundings. I'm in a clearing. A round patch of flat snow and solemn tree trunks. They're black, mossy, and checkered with uneven bark. In front of me, slightly downhill, is a pool of black water. It must be warm. It must be from an underground stream. I had heard about them. Like everything else I'm seeing right now, I'm witnessing it for the first time. The world was bigger than I thought. It couldn't have been any smaller for me behind the walls.

The water is dark, but clear. I'm leaning over it. In the bottom of the hole, there are piles of round stones. They go up, down, left, and right. Something is scribbled on them. Words. Names. I can't get a clear view of them. The water is moving. It must flow and enter someplace. Why do I need to know?

I bend over the pool and go down to my knees. I reached into the water. Why am I doing this? I need to move. I need to get to the shore. The Ills are waiting for me. The shore will be stormed. The second wave is coming. Everyone is certain of it. I'm certain of it. When will they arrive? What monsters will they carry? How will I match them? I've never fought for anything in my life, except to be loved.

That had not been successful.

For a quick second, deep in my brain, I hear the man's voice again.

"The sword will love you," he whispers.

I shake it away. It isn't like moments before. It isn't a real conversation. More of a fragment. More of a feeling than anything.

I'm holding a rock. It's round, flat, and smooth. I play with it in my long, white fingers. I took off my gloves. They gave me black gloves with padding and grips to hold the sword. They said I wouldn't need them. The Ancients are certain of my ability to adapt and change. They don't know me. We had never met until the ritual. How do they know that I will do this?

I have a small stick in my right hand. I'm carving. I'm cutting. The stone is soft enough for me to mark it. I'm surprised by my strength. I only know one thing to write. I know only one thing to put. Nobody tells me to. I feel a naturalness to it. I feel compelled to, as if I'm honoring something beyond. The name. My name, Catrina, is what I left on the stone. I play with it at my fingertips. I feel the divots. There are small dust trails where the material pulled apart under the tip of my branch. It blows away. It mixes with the snow-winter air.

Endless flurries. Unlimited snowflakes. In the city, which seems far away now, like at the bottom of a sea, it was never this cold and this snowy.

I drop the rock into the pool.

It floats for a second, then sinks onto the pile with the rest of the words. I blink twice, stand up, and tighten my gloves.

Why did I do that? What was the point of it? I started to move. I started walking here.

I run.

The Shingles

The island is smaller than our reports had originally stated.

At least the inhabited portion. I know this Cursed Island is mostly mountain, but even the settled part seems crunched and claustrophobic. I can't think of a single comparison in the Plains. There must be someplace to match this combination of isolation and suffocation.

I've been everywhere.

I've hunted dozens of landscapes. Dessert, islands, arctic, woodlands, even dust from the petrified forest has been cleaned out of the tip of my claws. That troll-haven is thick with death. The ground rumbles and bounces to their feet. There are many places I would not like to see again in the Empty Plains.

The petrified forest is only second to this haunted winter wonderland.

I think about those stone trees often. The cracked and dusty limbs spread in every direction. The brown, red, and sometimes purple marks of their rocky skins. Their occupants, too. The trolls. They were nearly extinct when I was sent there. There used to be thousands. They'd wander out of the woods when settlers appeared. They were ugly little settlements. Flat, unremarkable squares lined-up and stacked with no originality or uniqueness. Having traveled as much as me, to so many different roads and boulevards, you appreciate it when a city has a sense of self. It isn't just a shelter. It's an identity, a community. Without that blood flowing through the beast's body, there is no heart pumping. The trolls ransacked the city, stealing all forms of people away, but especially children. It liked the softness and suppleness of their bones and skin. The trolls were old. Not many had the right teeth left for eating grown men and women. The old were always safe. Not even monsters like that cut of meat.

Ironically, some of the trolls hated their own antiquity. They lived for centuries. Some were even glad when I, and the other hunters hired for their extermination, killed them. Not all were like this, but some. We slew them all. The entire race. I think. Behind our blasts, arrows, swords, and claws. They were so incredibly violent. Every animal, humanoid or not, gets vicious when confronted with their mortality. It's a song I've heard played a thousand different times, with a variety of instruments, melodies, and orchestras.

Back to the Cursed Island, my current hunt, my immediate objection. If you live in violence. If you make a past and present of it. Then, it is paramount you must always stay in reality. There is nothing more certain than the sight of blood. It comes for you once you've spilled it. There are a million eyes on this island who would love to watch me die. Father reminded me of that in the Plains. He said once you commit to being a hunter, you will in turn be hunted. Strip away the innocence of the world with your claws, well, death will always be in your shadow, waiting for the right moment to strike. I just need this last one. This last hunt. This final attack and confrontation. It is all I need. Then I am done. I can rest. I will be far away from this Cursed Island.

I reached the Shingles far too quickly.

They were occupied. Both Ills and townsfolk were planted along their tops, bottoms, and surrounding hills and woods like wandering mushrooms. They look odd in our armor. The Ills have their own crumpled, black-platted shells. They fit poorly, and are too small for their bulbous green bodies, or too big. They're easy to hear because they're constantly scraping or brushing against something as they march or perform other duties. The townsfolk looked even more ridiculous. They were a hodgepodge of armor, from both the Ills and our dead troops from the first invasion. Many of them carried our swords, crossbows, and shields. Some had curved swords and axes of the Ills. They have black handles with red feathers. They initially look crude, but they are stout and sharp. I assumed the feathers were ornamental, but they're meant to distract and confuse.

I learned this through experience.

Before I got close to the Shingles, I came upon a patrol. They were in a thin part of the forest, before the white hills and plateaus opened to the rocky teeth of these endless walls. There were seven Ills and three townsfolk. I killed them all. I used my third claw on a chain. Before they even noticed me, I was in the center of them, having dropped out of a tree. It wasn't hard to climb it. The trees are perfect for hiding. The bark is clingy, but sturdy. I used my second claw to pierce and hook its skin. I felt bad about it.

The claw spun in a circle three times, colliding with their faces and throats. It severed four of their heads and slit three of their throats. One of the Ills I struck below the chin too shallow didn't die right away. He spun, gurgled, and twisted about as the blood spurted from his flailing body. Two townsfolk and an Ill rushed me, pushing their dead and dying comrades out of the way. I kicked both townsfolk in the head with my left boot, between the slashes of their swords and parries of their shields. It broke their necks instantly. No need to dull my claws any more than I had too. The cold and endless snow would be hard enough on them already. I stood over their forms as they crumbled down into a paralyzed fog of eventual death.

It wouldn't be long.

I felt their spinal cords snap and twist, like a loose tree branch with just a small tendril of bark keeping it attached. The final Ill runs away. I swung my third claw out on its chain and carved the back of his legs. No armor there. Nothing to stop my scratches and talons. He collapses. I

74

approach slowly. He twists at me throwing a dagger. I'm impressed. I catch it out of the air with my right hand and hide it beneath my cloak.

I'm impressed. I cut deep. Not enough to kill, but far inside to cloud his mind with pain. He could still concentrate. No wonder the Ills unifying with the Diamond Town has blossomed into such an issue.

"I'm going to kill you, but I want to ask some questions first," I tell the Ill. It's older, lean, hobbled with blemishes and scars on its jade skin.

"Then why would I answer them?"

"Because there are a variety of unpleasant ways to die. There are also a variety of pleasant ways to die. I'm familiar with both. I can execute both efficiently. You have control over this situation in whether you'll share with me information about the island," I said.

The Ill wiggles a bit away from me. His armor clunks and crunches on the rocky snow.

"You speak my language," he asks.

"Yes, of course, you're not some foreign country here. The Empty Plains, just southwest of this island, used to be a part of your culture. Language is the same between it all. At least most of it. There are some variations of course, depending what part of the Plains you're from, but overall, it's pretty uniform."

I walk towards him and slightly kneel. Black blood leaked out from his shivering legs in wet ribbons.

"However, I do not have time for a history lesson."

The Ill snorts and chuckles. He's using his elbows to elevate his torso; he turns on his side in a more casual posture.

"How do you plan to kill me?"

It is my turn to laugh.

"I'm going to use this knife you threw at me. I'll stab you through the brain. I can't use my claws. I can't dull them. This is a long campaign. I'll need them to skin those Ancients in the city. This is a quick death. You won't feel a thing," I said.

The Ill is silent.

"What is your name?" I ask.

"Richa," he replies. His voice is tight and stumbling with pain.

"Richa, you have lost control of your life. However, you can have control over your death. Would you like the dagger to the brain, or should I open your guts. Your dagger isn't star metal. It won't cut cleanly. I'll have to really try."

Richa looks around. There is no help. There are empty stretches of forests and clearings all around us. We're on the edge of the Shingles. Further into their rows of broken teeth of rock and mortar, Richa might have reason for optimism.

"What do you want to know?" Richa said. He blinks his black eyes. Some Ills have white eyes, and others black. It is a major difference for the same species.

"Do the townsfolk know about the monster from the stars that fell here years ago?" I ask.

"No," Richa replies.

"Do you know?"

"Yes, it is in our books and lore. We were active long before this island was settled. We've tried to communicate with them about it, but they're polluted by the Ancients. Hence why the Guardians have hunted us for years. It wasn't until this last one that there was a change."

"I've heard. Sounds like quite a fellow. How'd he see past the curse of the sword?"

Richa shakes his head and gnaws on his lip. He's almost in shock. I'll have to kill him soon.

"We don't know."

I nod my head. I handle his dagger. I'm running out of time.

"Do Ills have the same sex organs as men? Or humans? Whatever way you want to refer to us?"

Richa trembles with pain and blinks. They're rapid, forceful blinks. He might be losing consciousness.

"What?" He asks.

"You heard the question."

A new level of paleness crosses his face. I lean close to him with the knife.

"I'm going to castrate you to expedite this conversation."

I'm not actually going to, never have, and never would. I'm no butcher. The threat is an empty box that nobody wants to look inside.

"You've only asked a few questions?" Richa stammers.

"Your answers aren't very impressive, though."

"The city doesn't know about its past, or the monster from the sky. The Ancients have kept them in the dark. They control everything that happens in that city. Everything. Even now, with our help, they look at us like rats. Our king and prince are tired of the hatred and killing, they bailed out the city from your mechanical invasion. Still, we're just rats. Do you have rats where you're from outlander?"

"There are rats everywhere," I replied.

"They calculated helping would be better than having you and your war machines on our doorstep."

Richa stops and swallows hard.

"None of it matters now, I'm on the other end of a dagger's point."

I threw that very dagger at that moment. I've dug far enough. The grunts don't have any real information to give. It pierces his green skull. It flies through his forehead and out a bursting slit behind his ears. There is blood, brains, bits of bone, but not a plethora of it. This isn't a blast wound. I didn't mean for it to go completely through. I underestimated the weight of the weapon. It shutters and clangs against the rocks behind him. He gurgles and fully collapses. I blow a bit of air out the corner of my mouth and sigh.

I don't know exactly what is ahead of me.

Our intelligence and spies, which have infiltrated since the Guardian was killed, said that Ancients are still distant despite having brokered a treaty with the Ills. They won't tell people what is going on beyond their obscure rituals and movements. They have a cathedral, hidden in the mountains, which is my target. The commanders think they'll have my answers and pieces there. I hope they're right. I'm not scared of any of these confrontations on an individual level with the Ills or townsfolk. In large groups, my advantage dwindles, so I need to reach the cathedral with the utmost stealth and secrecy. The Guardian, wherever she is, will be a worthy opponent. Not these green monsters. Not these civilians. I will not refer to the citizens as soldiers. They're not. They're substitutions and nothing more. I almost feel bad for them.

Almost.

That mindset can never be fully adopted. If I thought about it. If I broke the rocky gate behind my ribs open, to where my very human heart still beats, there would be too much guilt and pain to live. I have killed so many. I have done many terrible things. There is no going back. I have come too far. Once this island is complete and the monster's pieces are gathered for the mad scientist, well, I'll try it.

I'll try to have a normal life.

It isn't possible from where I'm standing now, on the doorstep of the Shingles, with a pile of the dead in my shadow. Each one, each kill that my claws have kissed takes a piece out of me. I wonder if there will be anything left when I'm back in the hills. Will the hounds want to chase me in the woods? Will the phantoms find me? Will Richa find me? Will I see him again as I toss and turn over a sweaty pillow before dawn has peaked over the faraway mountains? There is no answer. I want one, but I need to get there.

I move.

I'm running. My cloak bounces. My boots smack. My shoulders jiggle with my hidden armor. My buckles tremble. I'm alive at this moment. I need to focus on it. They taught us this when distracted by outcomes and futures to focus on the sensations of your body. The frigid air brushing past you. The crunching of frost and soil. The smell of metal, blood, and the sweat off my body. Stay present.

Distractions are the point of an arrow, the curve of a sword, and the tip of a knife.

I'm weaving through the trees and clearings closer to the slabs of rock with their crumbled ramparts and tilting foundations. The forest is thinner around their stone roots. The light is cloudy, which is good for shadows. It helps me. They said the weather never changes. Something to do with the fiend that fell from the sky. I don't know about any of that. There are plenty of landscapes across the plains where the weather stays consistent. Sure, there are small seasons only noticeable to local inhabitants, but to a visitor it can feel the same. This place might just be cold, regardless of the supernatural imprint from above.

I hear voices. Many. Both Ill and human. They're lost and muddled in the breeze. I'm fully in the Shingles. I duck, stop, then run again. I repeat. I follow every sound to where it might be ahead of me. I stop between two crooked teeth. I scale the side of the one on my right, using my third and second claw for leverage. The chain attached to my third claw served as a rope I could toss upwards then anchor, crawl, and then throw again. Another repeat. Another process of sneaking and stalking. I could make a game of it. I'm endlessly repeating. Most people in my situation would be flushed with anxiety and fear. This is my job. It is second nature. Violence is my beginning and end.

I do not study the clock. I study the language of blood.

I get to the top quickly and without trouble. It is deserted. The ramparts are flat with broken bricks and squares along their edge. The sky looks the same color as the stone. Gray. Gray everywhere. There are no signs that anyone has been here. No ash from campfires, weapons, or food waste. I know the Ills and townsfolk have stationed on some of the Shingles, but some must be more hospitable than others.

There are rows and rows of these ugly, half-hazard slabs. They continue for miles it seems. Their uneven tops point and slant in every direction. What was the purpose of this formation? They are all assorted sizes and pieces. There are no connecting corridors and ramparts. Each chunk is solitary and fixed. Where is the defensive strategy? How would you man such disjointed structures? I'm no military strategist on a macro level, the micro is where I earn my scars, but the lack of planning and sense doesn't really mesh with what sleeps on this Cursed Island. From what we know about the founders, former scientists and explorers from the Empty Plains who investigated the crash site years ago, there were no architects or military strategists among them. If they've been living forever, who was stupid enough to design such a useless line of stone?

Maybe the centuries have made them senile.

I'm down the wall and back onto the ground. I cannot linger. That isn't my mission. It's the head. The head of the snake. I need to cut it off. Remove it before the land forces get here. If we kill the Ancients, it'll be hard for them to organize. Or so they say, the superiors. They'll be in some meeting room snug and safe on a boat a hundred miles away. Their wine will be sloshing in the glasses beneath each restless buckle of the ship. Kain will be making them laugh. They won't be here. They won't know Richa. They won't feel the cold. They won't see the graveyard or the Shingles.

I have a feeling we'll all be needed by the time this is over. Even the generals might need to hold a sword or crossbow. Just my stomach telling me it. No reason. No magic. Just guts and experience mixing into a vague assumption. Most of life is this sensation, regardless of our education, training, and upbringing. You rely on this unspoken force to guide you through life. Part of it might be your inherent identity. The other part might be the past and future ideations of your mind trying to live in the present. Or, it might just be some nameless force, which will never be discovered or identified by some scientist or philosopher.

What do I know? I'm just a trained killer. A hired, bloody hand.

I continue my zigzag path through the Shingles. I don't have a particular plan for my route. I know that if I keep it random and unexplainable, anyone who is trying to track me, which would be extremely rare in this case, would be delayed by my unpredictability. Seldom do I see anyone wandering through these towering squares. Occasionally an Ill or two, but they're clearly not interested in patrolling anything or being observant. It must be hard for them to help a city that has tortured them for decades. The Guardian would hunt them for sport. They would be just toys for his and his predecessor's villainy. Now, they're protecting the city from certain destruction. The irony on this island is as thick and consistent as the snowfall.

I notice no change to the personnel and groupings until I get to the actual city. I must admit, until I was on its doorstep, it was a confusing, and almost dizzying approach. The Shingles seem to spawn from beginning to end with no real variation. Then, suddenly, as if some spell had lost its mystical potency, there was the city, the Diamond Town, in its minimalist glory.

The legendary metropolis was underwhelming.

It was a cobblestone cluster of unremarkable roofs, walls, and chimneys. On its edge was a wide bend of the river that gleamed with cloud-light on the black and blue water. A few buildings stood taller and shorter than the rest. Their rooftop line was uneven. From the highest points, their lantern and torch glows spout a bit of orange and red. The distant outline of rubble and holes along the city line were evident. The previous invasion had gotten so close. I can feel how desperate they were. Right at the edge. Just beneath the shadow. How close. How close they were. It must've been a massacre. They had to have wondered why? Mowing down civilians as if they were wheat or corn. A wholesale slaughter of the city. No magic. Just another kingdom beneath their gears and arrows.

Behind the city sits a row of towering mountains. They're gray, steel, stone, and solid, just like everything else on this island. A bit of black crawls upward at their base. I know they call them the Black Mountains, but they're half-finished with this obsidian paint. If only the Ills had not interfered. That's their territory. If only they had stuck to their caves and passageways, I wouldn't even be here risking my life before I can have the claw removed. It stings. The wintry weather makes the metal wet and tight where it enters my forearm. Someone in the petrified forest asked me if the mounted claw ever hurt me.

"Only when I'm alive," I whispered to him, as we hunted trolls in the stone-leaf underbrush. I'm not sure how they even knew about it. I keep it hidden beneath my cloak. A blade I always wanted sheathed. I can't remember him, the one that asked me. We were crouched down, waiting for the ancient beasts to stop patrolling near their caves and clusters. He was some nameless grunt. A conscript or draftee. Someone from some poor nation and small town. I don't get too attached to them, the grunts. I'm always in the deepest and darkest maelstrom. The storm clouds are hard enough for me to avoid. They all get blown away in heaps of bloody armor and broken shields. They're pawns and I'm the entire chessboard. I want to know them. I've tried. It is too much. A hefty distraction. Anything and everything can take your gaze.

I'll wait till nightfall before I enter the city completely. I'll want the dark. It'll mask me enough for their guards. I am worried the Ills might spot me. They're accustomed to the gloom. They were raised in it. That's their natural state. It doesn't matter. I can claw them apart like poor Richa and his ragtag patrol. I would just prefer not to. There doesn't need to be needless killing. Not that any of it is needed. You spend enough time swimming in the rivers of blood, and you realize you're on a boat with no captain.

War is a mess.

Hidden Oaks

A Rose for Walter

Despite there being a decomposing body in the guest bedroom of her two story, split-entry home, Marjorie kept the rest of the house extremely clean. The hardwood floors were mopped, the curtains washed, the bathroom tile scrubbed, and the windows wiped. It wasn't just because her husband's dead body sprawled across her son's old bed. Marjorie had always been a hygienic person, but with the various insects, fluids, and smells that echoed Walter's death, she felt like her obsessive-compulsive behavior was at least a little bit warranted.

Marjorie didn't want her life to change when it did.

When she woke up and turned to him to say good morning a year ago, nothing replied. He'd died in his sleep. She didn't know from what or how, but his blue eyes were fixed open at the ceiling like a fish on a cutting board. His skin was extra blue, the type that belongs in the sky. Her first reaction was to call everyone. 911. Her son. The coroner. However, she didn't want them to tell her it was over. She had a good imagination. She could keep Walter alive inside of it. She could always be far away from whatever was near, no matter how sad it was.

At first, she thought she could leave his body in bed with her. She could just pretend he was sick and bring him tea, crackers, and tissues. However, the smell started quickly. A sour, fleshy aroma that seemed to stick to your own skin. He also voided his bowels, which oozed through the mattresses and onto the floor in a brown puddle. She didn't know a lot about decomposition when she started this whole project, but she did know that she had to keep him in one of the basement bedrooms where the various fluids could seep through the spare bedding and into the floor.

Marjorie was a little concerned that the neighborhood might start to notice the stench or strangeness of the situation. It was easy enough to hide Walter's death. Nobody was interested in her or him. They had one son, Greg, who lived in Arizona and would only call them a few times a year. He'd gotten a job down there after college and made it his home ever since. He had a wife, but no children. Marjorie thought this was

82

an indictment of them, and she was right, though Greg would never tell her that directly in this lifetime. Marjorie always secretly hated how hard they were on their son. Walter would inspect him like a drill sergeant whenever he left the house. Teeth, hair, fingernails, clothes, all of it went under her dead husband's microscope. Greg never grew up with much confidence.

His wife had said once that he never felt good enough. Those words stuck with Marjorie. She didn't want to know why, but she did.

After Walter's death there were a few things, she didn't have to worry about anymore. Urine on the bathroom floor was one thing, along with being able to spend money on whatever she wanted. She didn't have to worry about him critiquing her driving, how well she dusted, or what she spent her time doing. There were countless fights when Greg was growing up about what kind of housework she'd do while he was working. Occasionally he'd do a white glove test to areas of the kitchen. It made her feel sick when he'd do that. He stopped following one occurrence when she stopped speaking to him for months.

Now, Walter was the silent one.

There were times when she missed him. The kiss on the cheek from his dry lips when he left for work in the morning. The box of chocolates on Valentine's Day. They way he fearlessly smashed bugs with his slipper. Now, insects had the last laugh. If only Walter could see what kind of palace his pale and withered body had become for them to play inside.

The last few days had been a little strange to Marjorie. She knew something serious had happened in the neighborhood because an ambulance had made a visit to one of her neighbors up the street. He was an older man with two children, grown and gone. She watched through her curtains as they loaded him into the back of the vehicle, blared the sirens, and shot down the road like an angry wasp. She'd never spoken to the man. He was far more of a hermit than her. His backyard was full of junk the few times she'd walked by his house. She remembered craning her short neck and adjusting her glasses so she could peer through the wooden fence. Rust, random shapes, and piles of miscellaneous equipment stared back at her.

When they took her neighbor away on a stretcher, she planned her trip to the mailbox at the same time. She waddled out there without directly looking up the street. She was wearing navy blue sweatpants and a black sweatshirt with white sneakers. She rarely changed out of them, with the amount of cleaning she needed to do at home. Plus, she didn't want to stain any of her nice clothes with bleach.

The walk back to her door between rose bushes and lines of bricks seemed longer than usual. It was like the path of concrete squares beneath her feet were popping up one after the other. She felt as if she was being led somewhere. There was a weird, sour smell blowing around the summer air. Maybe a pond that she'd never noticed had just taken a stinky breath. Sound seemed to be disjointed, distant. Sunlight had lost its edge. Then, she was at her door. She opened it slowly just to get her bearings. Her house was quiet. She stared at the black, metal rails that went upstairs and downstairs along white, carpeted steps. Downstairs was a dark hallway with three doors that led to a seldom used second family room, and there, just then, a brown door gently shut.

Marjorie blinked her green eyes as if they might tell her something.

Did she just see someone close that door?

That was where Walter's body was stored. Marjorie sat down on the steps and tried to look at the mail. Early on, after he had died, she noticed little things like this happening. She thought it was just part of the grief process, and they eventually went away. This moment was the first where it seemed like something strange had happened in this reality. If she'd had a dog or cat, or anything else living in the house they might've noticed it too. She could have a cat now that Walter was dead. He wouldn't let her have any pets before; they were too dirty, he said.

Marjorie stayed perfectly still on the stairs. She thought if she didn't move that perhaps the sound would return and she'd hear it again, maybe even surprise it, as if the mystery was a person. There were no other sounds in the house. Just the hum of the central air, the grumble of the refrigerator, and the occasional metallic coo of the wind chimes hanging outside her patio door. She could hear her own breath and the ticking of the grandfather clock upstairs by the couch.

"Okay, I really am just imagining things," she said, walking up the stairs.

"No," a voice said from somewhere. It was withered and distant, like it was hidden behind a hundred different walls.

"Hello? Hello, is someone there?" Marjorie said. Nothing replied.

"Okay, I'm really going nuts," she said, walking to the bathroom.

Later that day Marjorie had a tough time going anywhere in her house without stopping and listening. She still felt like someone was in the house with her, but there could be nobody else. She even popped her head into Walter's room, and sure enough his dried, pale body was tucked beneath the blanket where she'd left it. She did notice the doorknob was a little wet, but that could've been the moisture in the room brewing from his decomposition.

"I think I'm losing it," she said, as she closed the door on her husband's sour, dead body.

For dinner that night Marjorie warmed up a TV dinner and ate it on a metal tray in front of Wheel of Fortune. She liked the roast turkey with gravy, a bit of stuffing, and the Styrofoam-like mashed potatoes. A few bites into her meal and she heard another click of the door downstairs. She paused. She wanted her imagination to catch up with her. There were a few quakes of weight traveling in the house on the stairs and walls. Something was moving downstairs, it had to be. Marjorie stood up holding her plastic fork like a sword. She searched for words, but could only say one thing:

"Hello? Is someone there? How can I help you?" She said with a tremble.

She shook her head. Why did she sound like a cashier at the grocery store?

Nothing replied.

Marjorie stood up and walked over to the top of the stairs. She leaned over them, craning her tiny body against the black rails that followed each step. She didn't want to look too closely at the pocket of darkness where the basement started. It was alive, flowing, a piece of shadow from some unnatural abyss.

"He-hello?"

There was a strange melody, a song was playing somewhere in her house, but she couldn't hear it. The house seemed to stretch underneath her feet. The sensation reminded her of being on an Outrigger Canoe on their honeymoon in Hawaii. Walter was so adventurous then, she thought. He hadn't been ground down into routine, working for the ford plant in Saint Paul. This memory seemed to settle Marjorie and she steadied her legs. The house was back to normal. The temporary ocean had passed. The air smelled of evening light. The refrigerator buzzed lazily in the background.

"I think I'm ready for bed." Marjorie said. She threw away her dinner, turned off the television, wiped down the kitchen with some bleach, checked the carpet for crumbs, and closed all the blinds, curtains, and windows. She then crawled into bed. She listened for more sounds to echo up to her. She was hoping that the pink quilt wrapped around her body would act as some sort of fortress and make all the creepiness of the basement bounce off her. It reminded her of being scared when she was little. She'd hide underneath the blankets with her sister when the wind would howl too loudly.

For a while Marjorie couldn't sleep. She just stared at the windows to the left of her queen-sized bed. The blinds were pulled down over them in plastic tongues. Bits of sunlight crawled in around the shadows. A memory flashed into her mind of putting her son to bed during the summer, when the evening light was still a yellow edge aching around the window box. He'd cry so much about not being able to play with his friends, but Walter wouldn't budge an inch on it. If only Greg knew that his father was dead. Maybe that would bring him back here. There'd be no reason to stay away, even if she'd been complacent to it all. Walter scared her most when his routine was knocked off track. He was a delicate train that couldn't handle a single gust of wind. There'd be bruised knuckles and bloody noses to pay if he had to pause his life. Greg probably dwelled on those moments the most. Maybe he'd be happy to know she'd kept his father prisoner on the other side of life. It made her happy knowing that in the end she had all the control. He couldn't survive it.

That night she had a strange and particularly vivid dream. She was in some sort of prairie out west. It looked like North or South Dakota, but she couldn't be sure. It had been years since Walter took her anywhere but Duluth to watch as the big ships came into the harbor in the summer. Wherever it was she was imagining, it was empty of all things. There were billowing fields of wild wheat, grass, and flowers all around her. They were heaving violently. The rippling winds didn't touch, graze, or dent her presence. The scene reminded her of a painting Walter had been working on not long before he died. He'd given it to a neighbor for some random reason.

Marjorie couldn't completely feel her body though, she could just feel an image of herself being projected onto the scene. There was also a smell around her too. It was earthy, sunken, pond water she'd smell when it rained too much, and liquid would stand in pools between the blades of grass in her backyard.

Why would it smell like such decay in such a vivid scene, Marjorie thought?

Beyond the winds, wildernesses, and the fields, the sun was exceptionally blinding. There were no clouds at all. The blue slab of sky was standing over her. It filled in every empty detail in her vision.

Except for one thing.

Ahead of her, between the mounds of glowing yellow and green, was a bridge. It was cobblestone, with bits of moss on its dark base. Beneath it, where the water rushed by like it had no interest in whatever phantasm was blossoming, a shape was coming toward her. There was a sudden vacuum of air around her body in the direction of the shadow, pushing her closer as it grew out of the water into a flowing, half-absent figure. The way it bobbed and grew in the wind made her shudder and squeal. There was a pain between her bones and skin. Her body was coming apart. Eventually, the phantom was standing directly over her, dwarfing out the blue sky and glowing world around her.

Then, Marjorie awoke.

She'd peed herself. She could feel the warmth down her inner thighs to her feet. The blankets were heavy and wet below her legs. It had been years since something like this had happened. She panicked and quickly thrashed to get the sheet off of her. There was a slapping sound as her heel hit something directly behind her. She froze at first, her body couldn't communicate with her brain. She simply concentrated on breathing.

Marjorie had been sleeping on her side, as always, she hadn't even noticed someone else was in bed beside her. It was a human shape, also turned on its side. In the gloom of distant moonlight and morning darkness, she couldn't discern many details. Its skin appeared black and hanging, with bits of white weaved through it. It was wearing something too, some sort of pajamas that seemed familiar to her. There was a smell in the air. It was the same sourness that drifted through the house. She had tried to scour, scrub, wash, and wipe it away countless times with a whole shelf full of chemicals. Marjorie screamed and rolled out of bed. She scuttled back into a shelf, knocking photos and books down. A raspy voice rose up from the thing. It sounded stretched and barely there. It was trying to make itself work, but only solitary emptiness powered its vocal cords.

"Hello, honey," the voice said.

Star Ocean Foods

By the end of summer, Will was ready for school to start. He wasn't necessarily good at it. He had the uncanny ability to maintain a level of mediocrity that would be unnoticed by his teachers in both positive and negative ways. There were only a few subjects he enjoyed, and he zeroed in on those as if he were a pixelated missile launcher from Goldeneye. The rest of his classes were lucky to survive in the wake of this passion.

Will tried to escape the doldrums of late August by biking around his neighborhood. His grandparents lived down the road from him and he'd usually swing by their house for some pizza rolls and to watch their television. They had cable, and he loved to watch Nickelodeon, which would have reruns of Rugrats, Ahhh! Real Monsters! and Doug played throughout the day. One of his favorite shows, Salute Your Shorts, would sometimes be on as well. Watching that program made him jealous of the kids experiencing summer camp and the adventures they had. That type of life seemed a long way from where he was living.

On this afternoon, Will decided to skip the five-block trip to his grandparents and go a little bit further to Moore Lake Plaza. It was the classic late summer day. Slow and ambling cloud-shadows drifting across the empty driveways. Trees tilting on the breeze, looking so overgrown and lush, they almost looked fake, like toys in a train set. Sunlight was caught in beams over asphalt, flickering just enough to mimic a pool of tropical water on some sapphire beach. In the background was the buzz of power lines, cicadas, and the omnipresent 694 freeway.

For fun, Will would count the people he'd see at their houses as he biked. The suburbs always seemed empty until the evenings or the weekend. Next year at this time, Will would be old enough for a job, a prospect he both dreaded and relished. He was looking forward to the independence of having his own money to buy the latest Final Fantasy, but he was also dreading being away from his friends or talking to people. The older he got the more he realized that growth constantly came at a price, which irritated him.

Will was riding a maroon Huffy Mountain Bike with stars of rust along its handlebars. He'd left it in the rain a few times when heading over to his friend Darius's house. He didn't care if it looked a little eroded; it was more realistic to what he put the bike through. Plus, it upset his father when he didn't take care of his stuff properly. Anger was one of the only honest emotions his dad ever showed, so stroking it with small bits of negligence made him feel noticed and not invisible. Will was wearing black cargo shorts with a tan polo shirt. His curly hair was getting long and tangled. He'd have to get a haircut soon. He hated that. He disliked the mundane statements of people asking:

"Hey, did you get a haircut?"

Or.

"You look different today."

Often, Will would have whole volatile conversations back and forth in his head during these observations. He just wanted to tell people, "If you noticed I got a fucking haircut, then I got a haircut, stop fucking pointing it out. Use your goddamn deductive reasoning."

On the way to Moore Lake Plaza, Will decided he needed to avoid his grandparents' house. He could still ride by Hidden Oaks, but he needed to take a left or right at some point to bypass their home. He loved his grandparents desperately, but if they saw him ride by without stopping to say hello, they'd throw some guilt his way at the next family dinner over a plate of pot roast and gravy. If he stopped talking to them preemptively, they would insist he come inside and feed him a ridiculous amount of food to weigh him down forcing him to stay in the basement playing Warcraft 2. Complete avoidance was his only option.

As he glided by Hidden Oaks Park on his bike, something strange happened. He was pedaling along, listening to the hum and occasional crack of his tires pressing over pavement and miscellaneous rocks, when something struck his front wheel, sending him over the handlebars cartoonishly. He managed to roll his body up to absorb the impact, eventually crumpling on the curb like a frightened pill bug. During this crash Will did manage to let out one long and garbled:

"What the FUUUCCKKKKK???"

After getting to his feet, he looked for whatever he had hit. Last summer, Will had been biking while talking to his buddy Darius and ran into a parked car. This violent sensation echoed what he'd just experienced, only there was empty air where the collision had occurred. Will stared at his bike, back at the road, back at the bike, then back at the road. He turned to the woods next to him, which were parallel to the park, church, and playground across the street. He felt for a second, that the forest was watching him. A stranger through a bedroom window. Then he got angry, his most common emotion, and shook his arm at the forest.

"What the fuck dude?"

Will knew these trees well enough. Until recently he used them to hide from bullies. The thought poked a fresh, emotional bruise. He'd heard that Aubrey's house had burned down. Since then, he had not noticed her around, which was fine by him, until he biked by her old home a while back. The house was a charred skull atop a black, scorched hill. It bothered him to look at it. There was something eerie about the air hovering around its soot-etched sides. A feeling of profound hopelessness filled his heart as he stared. The burned-out abode was the very personification of sadness. It was only standing a few more days before a bulldozer plowed it sideways into a crumpled pile.

Back on the bike, Will zigzagged between quiet curbs and sidewalks towards Moore Lake Plaza. He rarely stood up on the pedals as he rode along. He was worried after his earlier crash over empty air. Maybe there was something wrong with his bike? Plus, he was not good at balancing in general, which showed with his shaky legs. Apparently, he was missing some tendons in his legs, but his parents could not remember which ones or how it affected him. He just knew he had a harder time doing things than other people.

Moore Lake Plaza was a long, L-shaped strip mall with a blue tiled roof, tinted windows, and a variety of stores, which divided the face of the building into various signs and advertisements. The building was remarkably flat. There was one exception; a large, empty building closer to its center where Grand Slam used to be located. This rectangle towered upwards like a wizard's keep. Will had a tough time focusing on the building with the sun reflecting off every surface, plus the heat off the concrete. He hadn't noticed the temperature as much until he had arrived. It was not surprising since it was still summer, but the gusts of furnace air were certainly worse at the strip mall than on the ride over. Even stranger, the parking lot seemed extra-long to bike through. It was some sort of mirage or wasteland, with just a few seagulls bothering to occupy this vast space.

"I don't remember it being this far," Will said, looking around.

There were multiple places Will loved to visit in the strip mall. One was the restaurant Joe DiMaggio's, which his family would go to often. The hobby store on the opposite end of the building had served as a go-to destination for model cars and boats, both of which taxed Will's patience, but sounded good in theory. His favorite spot used to be the Grand Slam, but it was gone, off to another neighborhood where other kids could save their quarters for a round of Killer Instinct or the batting cage. He could still remember the bass of the arcade's speakers thrumming through the neon green carpet and into his toes, vibrating the words "C-C-C-CCCOMBOOO BREAKKKER."

Will's destination today was the Asian grocery store called Ocean Foods, which was sandwiched between Joe DiMaggio's and a nail salon. The sign above the front windows, which were stacked high with bags of rice, was a bright, cobalt blue that always glowed with electricity regardless of the time of day. Will walked up to the doors and leaned his bike against the pillar just outside of them. The shade had a sharp, stoney coolness to it.

As he opened the door, a pair of metal bells with red ribbon clanged above his head. They echoed out onto the promenade, and that metallic sound seemed to immediately replicate, like a skipping cd. Will looked behind as if someone was following him, but the trapped strand of noise just repeated.

For a second, he was walking between a dream and reality.

Inside the store, Ocean Foods maximized every inch of space. It was not an exceptionally large establishment, just one long corridor of colorful stocked shelves, with a doorway on the right that led to a parallel room of similar scope. The shelves were square, ivory layers. On them was every variety of food that could possibly fit. Ramen, rice, noodles, sauces, produce, canned meat and fruit, coconut milk, curry paste, sardines, anchovies, jellies, candy, and verdant bamboo plants were just a few of these items. At the end of this vibrant tunnel of bright packaging was a glass desk with a single register atop it. Behind the checkout was a door with some shelves. The air smelled of lavender. A radio somewhere played cool jazz. It mixed in with the humming of refrigerators and coolers.

"Hello, William!" A voice said from somewhere in the back. It was Mrs. Lee. She was the store's owner. She inherited the shop from an uncle who had moved back to Thailand. Mrs. Lee was an accomplished piano player and teacher, hoping to retire in Canada with her husband in the next few years. She would sell the store once she got tired of it, which happened immediately after her uncle had called her about it. Customer service was not a natural fit for her personality, but she didn't mind Will stopping by two or three times a week.

"Your gum is on the counter, William. Take your time. As always," she said. Will smiled and started to make his way to the other room of the store.

Ocean Foods was Will's escape from the dullness of the suburbs. He loved everything about it. The vibrancy of the food, the diversity of language and design, and even the glow of the fluorescent light across the tiled floor. It felt like he was stepping into a different world, one so much more alive than his own. This snapshot into a different culture made him excited to experience life. Will usually bought gum from Mrs. Lee. There was a variety pack from Japan with orange, lime, grape, and a few other flavors. They came in small boxes, which were wrapped in cellophane with a red thread running through it.

Occasionally, he'd buy a bottle of Orbitz with gelatinous pearls of orange floating inside of it. This was the only store that still carried any because people could not stand the slimy consistency. His friends thought it was like drinking a lava lamp. He didn't mind it, and he knew it was on borrowed time.

As he went to reach for his beverage in a refrigerator in the middle of the room, a strange sound filled the store. It was like music, but shallower, as if it was there, but did not want to be heard. The room started to stretch out ahead of him as he tried to find the sound. His breathing quickened and he started to sweat, even though the temperature in the store was ridiculously cold. The building continued to grow, until the shelves looked so distorted, they resembled a tunnel of mirrors.

Will could now see himself, sweaty and shaking. He looked away from the image. Normally, on this side of Ocean Foods there was a small deli counter with live catfish just beneath it, swimming endlessly in a round tank. Instead, there were more reflections of himself. He started to panic.

"I'm, I'm, I'm all over the place!" Will screamed.

He started to run wildly but he did not seem to move at all. He panted and squealed, too afraid to lift his head and see the endless tiles of reality mimicking him.

"Come on. Come on. Go away!"

He looked up finally and saw that according to the reflection he was running sideways, but vertically in place on the floor. He screamed and stopped. There was a laughing hiss somewhere. The ground shook.

"Everything okay?" Mrs. Lee said from somewhere.

Will caught his breath and tried to relax.

"Yeah, yeah, I'm good. All good here," he said, watching his sweat dripping onto the floor.

Will took a few moments to recover from what happened. He couldn't explain it, but it felt familiar. Despite being severely unnerved, Will wanted to get some Pocky before he left, and started to walk further down the hallway to where a row of glittering, crimson boxes were stacked. He stopped as he reached for it. There was something wet dripping on his head. He gazed upwards to find raindrops pelting his face and eyes. There was a gray, uneven sky above him, with strands of dark clouds billowing. Tendrils of lightning sizzled into themselves with bony trails of snapping light. Thunder trailed their sparks in a hollow drum roll, shaking his rib cage.

Will could not comprehend what was around him.

He was no longer in Ocean Foods, but an alley in another country. There was an oily mix of streetlights and illuminated signs of Kanji, which hovered just above his shoulders. The air smelled salty and fried. Rooftops were scaled and tiled, dripping with rainfall. There was a cacophony of cars buzzing, conversations mumbling, and pots boiling. Will took a slight step backwards in shock, and was suddenly back in Ocean Foods, reaching out toward the rows of Pocky.

"What, what the hell is happening?" Will said, patting his hands on his chest to verify his physical existence. His clothes were completely soaked in water. His hair was drenched.

He even had some in his mouth that he spit on the floor in a panic.

"I need to go. I need to go." He said, grabbing his food and drink and staggering across the floor. His shoes were barely gripping the ground. He was simply hoping Mrs. Lee wouldn't notice the dripping pool following him.

As Will passed the fish tank, he stopped. He could hear the music again, the strange melody that wouldn't completely reveal itself to his ears. The catfish were large, whiskered, and a color that was a mixture of green and black. They gazed up at him through crusty, circular glass and opened their large mouths pensively, as if they were trying to speak. All around him, the world turned murky and cloudy.

Suddenly, he was floating in a massive expanse of open water.

He panicked and started to thrash. The sky was the same violent scene as the previous alleyway. The waves churned over his head. As one pushed him beneath the surface, he noticed the abyss below his scrambling feet. Pure and limitless darkness. The very definition of the word deep, was looking up at him. He pushed his head to the surface. A line of jade fins was coming towards him, unhindered by the froth and bending layers. Judging by their length and height, the fish was huge, a leviathan, unlike anything Will had seen on TV during Shark Week. As it closed in on him, he could see its mouth open into a living chasm of red muscle. It was centered by a pink tongue. The maw was so large he stared through it as if it were a tunnel. Deep in its gullet, as the jaws began to clamp over him, Will could barely see a row of pearl teeth sitting far inside. A monster within a monster. Will tried to swim away, but the fish clamped onto his arm, pulling him into oblivion below.

"William? What on earth are you doing with my fish?" Mrs. Lee said from behind the deli counter. She was wearing a navy-blue apron. Her hair was tied back in a red scrunchy that matched her lipstick. Her glasses were gold-rimmed and thin, and her eyes were wide with puzzlement.

Will screamed and tried to pull his hand free of the catfish's body. His whole wrist was inside it. He could feel parts of its throat, soft and slimy, mixing in with his fingers and knuckles. After a few disgusting seconds, he finally shook it off.

The fish dashed to the other side of its tank, feeling completely mystified and somewhat violated.

"What were you doing? You got water everywhere! You're completely soaked. And look at my store!?" She was too confused to be angry. This was completely out of character for Will.

"I, uh, I need to go now," Will said.

"Oh no. Oh no. You're not going anywhere until this is cleaned up. I'll go get my mop for you." Mrs. Lee said. Will stared at his wrist puzzled. Wrapped around his skin was a ring of ink with strange symbols on it. The markings sparkled in the fluorescent light. They looked fresh, unblemished, and his skin beneath them looked irritated. As Will focused on them, he could hear some dry laughter echoing far away, but still close enough.

The Butterfly

Trips to Hidden Oaks Park were a momentary respite in Donna's hectic day. Potty-training her two daughters. Making them breakfast, lunch, and dinner. Playing with them. Watching them. Putting them to bed. In fact, the afternoon walks to this small park called Hidden Oaks had become the only time her mind could catch up with the constantly moving world around her. The park, or more importantly the playground on its edge next to the church, was seldom used and mostly clean. Oftentimes, Donna and her daughters were the only ones using it.

In truth, this sanctuary of slides and ladders was a better partner to her in raising their children than her husband. It did not ask questions, judge her, or get upset if she was tired. It would simply play with her kids, quietly and confidently, without needing her guidance.

Donna was 38 years old. She was tall, with black hair, olive skin, and green eyes. She loved summers in the Midwest because it got hot enough for her to wear sundresses every day of the week. Her parents were from Portugal, and she had met her husband when she was going to the University of Minnesota for a degree in English Literature. He was an HR Specialist who would travel from state to state; hiring and firing people so companies themselves would not have to get their hands dirty. This made him extra confrontational at home. Literally any conversation could easily be fanned into a fight. Life was stressful, but still easier with him traveling.

It was a hot, August day when they saw it. That afternoon had the typical summer scenery; uneven clouds, humid wind, and bumblebees bouncing among the legions of dandelions along Hidden Oaks Park. Cotton Willows were still shedding their translucent, wispy skin into the air, which seemed unusual and unnatural for so late in the summer. When Donna arrived with both kids running alongside her stroller, stomping their feet and screaming at one another, the familiar sight of the wooden playground with a yellow slide and monkey bars was staring at them from beyond the hill and church near the entrance to the park. Both kids were magnetized toward it and sprinted in that direction.

Strangely, as Donna watched her children dash ahead, something appeared along the corner of her eye. Directly across from the old playground, seldom used baseball and soccer fields, was a brand new, brightly colored playground. Across the street from it was the small forest, tennis courts, and a hill.

"When... When did that get put in? I'm here every day." Donna said, mostly to herself. She couldn't help pointing at it as her brain arrived at this new information.

Her daughters noticed her gesture and immediately changed direction.

"Look, look mommy, a new playground," her six-year-old daughter Matilde screamed.

"I see that, wow, huh?" Donna said.

"Look, look," her four-year-old daughter Mariana said, following her sister.

"I know, I know I see it honey,"

The new playground was sandwiched next to a smear of trees and few random yellow poles marking a utility shed where lawnmowers and other park maintenance equipment was stored. The structure sparkled underneath the sun. It was a hodgepodge of red, blue, and black climbing pieces. Attached were swings, digging shovels, monkey bars, slides, wall puzzles, and ropes from which the children could dangle. It stood about 15 feet at its highest point, where a large, ruby slide would fire them to the ground through a plastic cyclone. The ground was covered in wood chips. Donna was glad there was no sand. There had been many times cats had left presents in the other playground, only for her daughters to find.

"Mommy, what is this, chocolate?"

They would not have that problem at this new playground.

"I still can't believe I didn't notice they were doing this, or putting this in," Donna said, watching her kids run headfirst to the glittering mass of childlike wonder. She was at the park nearly every day of the week. She would've noticed construction, a crew of people working, or even trucks hauling in the unassembled pieces. There was none of that to her recollection, but Donna wasn't always paying attention to these things. She was more concerned about sunscreen on her kids, whether they were fed, and how high they were playing on the equipment.

Donna watched her children crawl on the new playground all afternoon. It was hard to get them to come home when it was time to leave. They talked about it the entire way back. They sang about it at dinner, in the bathtub, and at bedtime. Donna even dreamed about it, but she didn't tell anyone about that experience. If her husband had been home that night, she'd have wanted to wake him up to talk about it. Of course, he'd likely only partially listen and just want to have sex, which was the exact opposite of what she needed.

The next afternoon when they walked down the road to Hidden Oaks, they were even more surprised.

Beneath the billowing drags of summer clouds, hot breezes, and random bugs, the new playground had expanded. Now, it was double in size, with two identical colorful structures standing next to one another linked by a wobbly bridge over the square of pulverized wood. They both looked the same, like a partial mitosis had occurred, but was interrupted. It was almost as if she was starting at a reflection.

"There's two now," Matilde said, running towards one of the slides.

She went up the red tube backwards, spreading her feet out to grip along the slick surface. It led to a black platform with holes in it. The material beneath her pink sneakers was bubbly and bouncy, unlike the old playground on the other end of the park that had wooden planks to walk along, which would sometimes give her splinters. Matilde was dressed in a white and pink sundress with flowers. She didn't know why her mom always dressed her up when they went out, but her mom said she looked so beautiful she couldn't help it. Matilde had blondish hair, but with darker skin, and her father's blue eyes. She had a round chin with a scab on it from falling on the walk home.

Matilde was bigger than her sister Marianna, so she could climb up on objects that her sister couldn't reach. Doing this could give her a vantage point from which to look out and better understand her surroundings.

She climbed on top of the slide and stood to look around the park. There was the utility shed, the hill, the nearby church, the older playground, a seldom used baseball field, and the old ice rink. The breeze was sticky, the grass glowed, and shadows beneath the trees trembled. She smelled the air and coughed. It stunk, like mud or pond water. It reminded her of the water that had filled up her father's wheelbarrow the time he had left it out in the backyard for a month. It was rancid and sour. It seemed to be coming from the slide itself, in fact all the equipment reeked of it.

Being up high didn't bother Matilde. She was a bit of a daredevil. Oftentimes she'd walk backwards down the road, despite her mother's screams and nags. While she gazed out over her vantage point, she noticed across the street a wedge of forest. Behind the trees, was a small pond with a speck of an island floating in its center. As her eyes focused on it, she could hear some strange music from somewhere. It echoed off the slide's plastic skin. The ring of brown water around this chunk of marshland seemed to rise upwards the longer she looked. It took over the horizon, ate up the forest, and silenced the wind. It pooled over the road in a relentless stain and splashed up against the stalks of metal holding up the playground.

Then, the water stopped and there was a hiss from beneath the brown waves. Toys, a whole plastic, and metal galaxy of them, floated up in bright, earthbound stars. Boats, cars, telephones, animals, dinosaurs, bikes, scooters, and even Legos, quietly hovered. She smiled and crawled down to the platform. She carefully went down the slide. She stopped herself at the bottom so as not to step into the water. Even if the toys were a bit yucky, she'd still be happy to have them.

"Honey, how long are you going to stand in that spot for?" Her mom asked, suddenly. Matilde blinked once and looked around. She was still on her perch. She looked at the woods across the street, then down at her feet in disbelief. There was no music, toys, or flood. She sighed and jumped down. She started to cry.

"What's going on honey?" Donna said, crawling up the playground ladder and across a wobbling bridge. Matilde was sobbing wildly.

"Where, where did all the toys go?" She wailed.

Marianna was now playing on the ground. She'd been making her mom hold her up to the monkey bars so she could grip them. Sensing the slight bit of freedom provided by her sister's tantrum, Marianna wandered towards the edge of the playground where there was a long stretch of trees that separated a home's backyard from Hidden Oaks. She started to balance herself on the lip of wood that separated the park's grass and the playground's wood chips. Marianna was similar in appearance to her sister, only her eyes and hair were dark, and she was wearing a white shirt with a Nickelodeon logo on it, and a frilly pink skirt. She had a bow in her hair, which beamed against her tan, smiling face. As she continued to wander along this divide, something drifted across her gaze.

It was a butterfly.

Only, it wasn't like any butterfly Marianna had ever seen before. It had a blue body with yellow wings and blank antennae. She looked for more details on its body, but she couldn't see any patterns or fuzziness to its form. The bug appeared to be forged out of light. It glowed, beamed, and bobbed in a magical gleam, as if it was from some sort of cartoon. It seemed to grow as she watched it, as well as vacuum up all the sound around her. She couldn't even hear her sister sobbing just thirty feet away. There was no shadow beneath the butterfly either; it just danced there a few feet away from Marianna's head.

"Wow, I've never seen anything like that before," she said in her tiny voice.

Something shifted next to her. It made the ground shake and trees rattle.

"Do you like it?" A deep, echoing voice said.

Marianna turned to the forest on her right. There was nothing there on first observation, just another small line of trees, bushes, and other bits of greenery. Then, as her eyes started to focus more on the pockets of air and sunlight between the branches, she noticed a large shape mixed into the foliage. She couldn't make out any of its details, but it was tall, wide, and bent. Her vision found what looked like a hand dangling down from the shadow. As the clarity of its form started to dawn on her, she suddenly smelled something foul and turned her head away. A vacuous silence followed, and it grew. It was piercing. She could practically hear her lungs making oxygen.

"I said, do you like it?" The voice said again.

Marianna stepped backwards.

There was a hiss somewhere and a flash of green light. The single butterfly instantaneously spawned into several, which bobbed on the wind just ahead of the girl.

"How about now?"

Marianna couldn't reply. She was hypnotized by the image. It was a living fairy tale. The whole rest of the world melted away like finger paint. She opened her mouth and started to drool.

"That's better," the voice said.

A yell broke the trance. Marianna's mother was looking for her. The butterflies suddenly flashed upwards in narrow streaks. They were being pulled into some otherworldly drain hidden in plain sight. The process made a thunderous sound that only Marianna could hear. She turned to the trees as the form vanished, as though it had stepped through some sort of secret door. The earth rumbled. Then it was gone.

"Marianna, Marianna, don't run off without me. We have to go; I can't calm your sister down. she's nuts," Her mom said, grabbing her by the hand.

"There were butterflies mommy," Marianna said, being led off.

"Yes, honey, butterflies."

Donna and her daughters arrived at Hidden Oaks the next afternoon with a slight bit of trepidation. Originally, that morning, Matilde hadn't wanted to go, but after exhausting every inch of their backyard playing, she'd forgotten her feelings of the previous day. When they got to Hidden Oaks, they stopped in disbelief before fully entering the park.

The playground was gone.

The lawn where it stood was empty. There was even full-length grass where the wood chips had populated the day before.

"Where'd it go mommy?" Matilde said, staring at the vacant bit of green.

"I, I don't know." Donna said, wandering towards the spot. There were no signs of tire tracks, construction, or anything else. She shook her head and almost blinked out some tears.

"It's gone," Matilde said.

Donna had to remain composed in front of her children, but in all honesty, she wanted to scream and rant. What happened was scary, weird, and completely unexplainable, but what was far more frightening for her was that she felt like she couldn't tell anyone about what had happened. Who would come close to believing her? She'd be alone with this nightmarish anomaly for the rest of her life. She didn't know what she'd tell her kids when they'd bring it up. She could just say something simple as it was taken away, but they wouldn't know the strangeness of it like she would.

"Are we still going to play at the park, Mommy?" Marianna asked.

"Yeah, yeah, let's go, but just for a little while today," she said.

As they walked back to the old playground made of splinter-filled lumber and poking slides, Marianna looked back at the forest across the street with the pond inside of it. A single, yellow and blue butterfly played in the air.

It drifted for a few moments to let the girl smile, and then vanished into the trees.

Factory 9

ATTENTION. SALVAGE AD. HIGH REWARDS

Tin One: Tin One's primary purpose was salvaging, specifically garbage collection. The width of its body, plus the plethora of storage compartments built around its core allowed it to carry copious quantities of inorganic and organic material with relative ease. Before the war, Tin One's were consistently helping with the Global Clean-up Initiative (GCI) but were waylaid due to the conflict.

You can distinguish a Tin One because of its large, round, garbage-can-like shape. They have a short head, red eyes, and feet with rolling treads. Their back has an exhaust square for venting. They have four arms, two along the sides, with two smaller ones in the middle. Collectors for the Reclamation Agency of Earth (RAE) will pay a hefty price for any refurbished or partially recovered models. They must include undamaged solar fuel cells. Expired batteries are okay. Damaged CPU is also acceptable.

If you know anyone who might have knowledge of this item or model, please contact your local RAE office for more information. It is imperative that we find one with undamaged fuel cells. It is essential to the history of our species.

Thank you.

Tin One

At first, there was nothing. Then, a flash of green light formed the edges of its vision, filling it with grids, numbers, and schematics of the tiny room surrounding it. Then there was a clicking sound, as the gears in its chest started to find themselves.

It was alive.

Next came more sight. The grid switched to red, black, then whatever the robot wanted. The room settled around it. The machine was inside some sort of utility closet with a variety of mops and brooms jammed against the doorknob in a wayward pyramid. The only light source was a small orb of illumination trembling just outside the red gems of its optical nerves.

There was another hum somewhere in its round body. The microphones hidden along its sides just opposite of its eyes clicked in static snaps. The feedback settled, and a small voice emerged from behind the beam.

"Shhh, don't talk. Be quiet. They'll hear you. They'll hear us. Lower your volume to whisper if you can. I think that was the setting."

The robot made the adjustment in its matrix before the sentence finished. Another speaker percolated in the brown plate where its mouth would be.

"State operator for point of reference," the machine said.

"Again, you gotta be quiet. You must be. They'll hear you and come in here. I don't think you're ready to tussle with the Phantoms just yet."

"Operator must be identified before the directive can be followed," the machine said. Its voice was like that of a human male, only hollow, lacking inflection, with sparks of feedback between words.

"What? Oh. My name is what you want?"

"Name, title, or position, whatever is most applicable to the waste management environment."

"Waste management huh? Well, the entire world is wasted, burnt, scarred, and toxic."

"Name, title, or position please?"

"Sorry, it's Raphael."

"Raphael, please state the desired inquiry."

"Oh, um, I don't have one yet, just be quiet. Being upstairs in the factory is risky. I don't think the Phantoms come down this corridor often, but we can't be too careful."

The sensors along the robot's eyes adjusted again in a small flash and it could see it was a human boy, around the age of 12. He was tall for his age, extremely thin, and had a mop of curly black hair that was tangled with debris. His hairstyle was like a permanently unfinished bird nest. He was dressed in a hooded sweatshirt with holes and rips on every section. Wrapped around it was a coat of a similar state. The machine's thermometer was blinking 45 Degrees Fahrenheit.

Raphael approached the wall and leaned his head against it. The pressure from his body's weight loosened some dust from the ceiling. It looked like snow against the flashlight. He looked back at the robot and nodded his head. His skin was as pale as fresh paper. It nearly reflected in the gloom.

"I, I think we're okay for right now. What should I call you, do you have a name?"

"Label Tin. Model number one. Please state the location for salvage operation," the robot chimed.

"Label Tin? Model one? So, the shortened version is Tin One?"

"Correct. Label Tin. Model number one."

"Let's go even less than that. We'll just call you TO if that's okay?"

"T? O?"

"Yeah, like 'to,' but TO. So, you were the first version of your model, do you have bugs or anything?"

"No. I have a corrective matrix. If errors occur, I have the ability to implement change and learn from problems. It is a basic component of all Chronos Technology," TO said.

There was a vibrating sound somewhere in the walls, followed by a thump. It made Raphael stare at the door. He wanted to see through it.

"Wait till you get a load of the problems out here," he whispered to himself. Raphael stopped, and promptly vomited onto the floor in a casual lurch. He shrugged it off, like it was as casual as a sneeze. His puke was white, chalky, and dotted with bits of blood. Only TO could see it in the dark.

"Onset radiation poisoning. Have you been diagnosed by a medical professional?"

"What? No. Not many of those around anymore. I've been puking since the sky went dark. I think everyone has, just part of the world we live in," Raphael said.

"Radiation poisoning can be fatal unless symptoms are treated. Would you like me to map out a route to the closest medical facility?"

"Ha, well, you could if you wanted, but I'm sure it is either a hole or completely empty or whatever. I suppose you don't really know what's going on outside."

"Outside? The origin of manufacturing was Industrial Blvd in Minneapolis, Minnesota. Is this not the same location?" TO asked.

"Oh yes, it is, but it may not be as memorable as the images given to you by your programmers."

"What is the date?"

"Sorry TO, I only know the year."

"What is the year?"

"It is 2071."

"Four years since my model was manufactured."

"Oh yeah? I guess that makes you the youngest in our group. Gabby will like that. He's never really liked being the younger brother."

"Gabby? Another human?"

"Yup, my little brother, he's back in the basement here. We'll head out shortly, I just need to catch my breath. Barfing is pretty common for me, but I still get tired from it," Raphael said.

"Would you like me to map out a route to the closest medical facility?"

"I'm good, I'm good."

"You do not seem good."

Raphael sat up straight and patted the round metal chest of TO with his hand.

"There is no good right now, only alive."

"I don't understand," TO said.

"You will once we get outside this mop closet, hang on a second," Raphael said. He turned towards the door again and pushed up against it. He pulled out a stethoscope from one of the ripped pockets along the side of his hooded sweatshirt. He ran the metal disc along the door.

"How good are your ears?"

"I do not have ears. I have infrared microphones installed along my cranium."

"Do they hear anything outside the door?"

"There is too much noise overall; ambient static from rain, wind, and something moving in the floor beneath us," TO said.

Raphael lifted both feet back and forth like he was trying to dance.

"Under us? What?"

"It is gone."

"Geez, must've been an insect. Maybe I don't want to know all the things you can hear," Raphael said.

TO spun its body back and forth like it was stretching for a workout video. It could rotate its torso 360 Degrees, which at first looked slightly demonic to Raphael. A few gears ached and howled against the stasis the machine had just been revived from.

"Keep it down! You don't want to draw anything up here to us. We never hang around the upper levels." Raphael squealed.

"I cannot help creating certain audible reactions from my form being activated," TO said.

"Do you have a silent mode or something?"

"I am capable of reducing sound, yes."

"Okay, do that. Do that now. I can't stress that enough."

"I must finish waking up my limbs."

"Seriously? What did I just say?"

"I cannot move silently without my appendages properly revitalized."

"Alright, just get it over with."

TO lift its knees in the air. The robot's legs were tree trunks, sitting atop little pyramids. They hissed bashful bursts of steam and oil. He then moved his arms, which were like branches, with round, hotdog-fingers poking out the ends.

"I am prepared." TO said.

Raphael sucked in a deep sigh and pulled the hood over his hair. His curls jumped out for a second before the fabric circled around his face.

"No, you're really not."

The door inched open slowly. Raphael peered around its white edge with a small mirror attached to a piece of pipe. He wasn't willing to put his flesh anywhere near the opening until he knew it was clear.

"A reflection?" TO chimed.

"Shhh!" Raphael hushed. He turned the mirror upwards to look at the ceiling.

"The Phantoms usually sit in the rafters like bats. Making sure they're not there," he whispered.

"Phantom Security Drones Mark 12?" TO said.

"Sure, those, I've never known their actual names. I just saw some signs on the walls about them."

Raphael stuffed the mirror into his backpack in one quick motion of his right wrist. He barely bent his arm. Using it was obviously second nature. He then grabbed a sawed-off shotgun with a single barrel. There were a bunch of words etched into the red wood of the handle.

"Remember, we must be quiet as we go out. Outside this door across from the cafeteria is a hallway. We're going to take that all the way down the stairs. Before we actually enter the stairwell, I'm going to throw a few rocks into the cafeteria to divert the phantoms. Then we'll go down the stairs. There is no way we'd be able to use them if the Phantoms weren't occupied. You understand?" Raphael said.

"Yes. I'm familiar with the building design. I have a blueprint saved and interfaced to my memory," TO replied.

"I figured."

When Raphael finally opened the door, the world staring at TO was nothing like any of the images in his hard drive. They were in a large room, which was completely dark except for a hole in the ceiling where rain was pouring through. The light from the toxic clouds gave the water a white glow, which illuminated the ground and the ocean of wreckage covering it. There was so much debris on the floor, TO couldn't relax his optical sensors to interpret it. Chairs, tables, ceiling panels, rocks, metal, dust, bones, and fabric were just a few objects spread across the tiles. On the left side of the room was a long counter covered in curls of shattered glass.

"You'll get used to the smell," Raphael said. He was crouched at TO's feet, using the robot's shadow as cover.

"I cannot smell."

"You're lucky then," Raphael replied. He shook his head. The smell of rot was everywhere. It was the dank and moldy type of decay, the kind that is wet and sour, and sits on your nose. It had smelled like this since the apocalypse started, which Raphael didn't even know when. He remembered going underneath the stairs with his dad to put Christmas decorations away and the floor had a similar stench.

"This way, move quietly." Raphael said, nodding towards a hallway opposite their hiding spot. There was a red light glowing atop the ceiling.

"Only thing left working after the Silent Ones woke-up and the military blew them up are the Exit Signs. Ironic isn't it. I most certainly want to exit this horrifying world." Raphael was taking small steps in front of TO, as if he was trying to walk on a wire.

"Silent Ones? I'm unfamiliar with them," TO said.

Raphael crept through the constellation of debris. He reached the hallway opposite the closet, then motioned for TO. The robot was still learning how to walk and in the forty feet it had moved since waking up minutes earlier, its legs wiggled and trembled under the weight of its can-shaped body. A streak of lightning cut the clouds outside the roof, throwing purple light between the shadows. Raphael motioned with the gun and fully closed his eyes. Not watching the newly awakened robot stagger between mounds of rubble was essential to maintaining his sanity.

After a few sweaty seconds, TO arrived at the entrance to the hallway. He towered over Raphael. It was the first time the 12-year-old boy had felt safe in months. Finding the salvage robot randomly in the broom closet was fortunate, but also finding a manual on how to activate the machine in one of the desks downstairs was a godsend.

"Get behind me, and I'll throw a few rocks across the cafeteria. They'll be here quickly. The moment they appear we'll run into the stairwell. Remember, I'll go first and just follow me." Raphael said.

He reached into his backpack and switched the gun for a small slingshot. He crouched onto the floor and rummaged for a few stones out of the shattered walls around him. Raphael stood up and jiggled a few rocks around in his hands. He remembered skipping stones with his dad on a lake shore years ago. Seeing the old green world, even in a haze-edged memory, made Raphael want to puke.

He slung both shots into the dark room. They crashed, clanged, and echoed against the gloom. Raphael sunk down into a crouch and pushed himself against the wall. His shotgun was back in his right hand. TO hadn't even noticed him switch it.

"Hide you fool!" Raphael hissed at TO. The robot quickly backed further into the hallway and into a ripped doorway with smears of black mold on its frame.

At first, nothing seemed to change in their environment. There was thunder outside. The trickles of water through gaps in the roof thrummed against random surfaces. The wind shook the foundation in repetitive howls.

Then, they heard them.

It started as a light hammering sound, but the closer it got the more it intensified. Something was smashing its limb into whatever mass it could find. Walls, ceilings, doors, pillars, anything with enough structural integrity to give the factory a good vibration was slammed. TO didn't like the sound. It crashed further into the empty room opposite the hallway. It was programmed to experience fear, or to be cautious of dangerous sounds. Both reactions were happening concurrently, which made it feel overwhelmed.

"They, the Phantoms, do this to intimidate people into moving before they appear. Just hold steady and I'll tell you when to run," Raphael whispered. Something clanged in the mess hall, a pair of shadows hung over the ground. They jolted with each step. They were tall, wide, and sharp. Their bodies were covered by some sort of fabric, which spiked around their shoulders and arms. Behind their cloaks were glowing lines of metal extensions, but Raphael couldn't make them out without getting distracted by the fear being produced by them. Whenever the Phantoms moved there was a wrenching sound, like the material supporting their bodies was stiff, and their atoms were squealing. They were an out-of-tune violin with no one to play for.

After a few minutes, the phantoms were against the opposite wall, just below the hole in the ceiling with the flashes of white rain clapping through.

"Okay, follow me," Raphael said. He crawled down the hallway on his knees, between cracked plaster and cement. TO follow noiselessly until they reach the stairwell. The door was ripped off its hinges. Raphael clicked a round dial on his wrist and a flashlight beamed on to a set of stairs. Raphael scampered down them, followed by TO. The robot hadn't walked on steps before. The sensation of going downwards was new and awkward. The first few tries were shaky and a little loud, but Raphael didn't say anything as the steam from his gears was released, the human must've understood how new everything was to the long sleeping machine.

They traveled down four flights, until they came to a basement door that was closed. Raphael clicked it open while keeping the white beam in front of him. The boy moved like a living searchlight. Cockroaches, centipedes, and other creatures scattered in the hallway they entered. Raphael shook his head and sighed.

"Wait until you see their big brothers and sisters," he gulped in the dark.

They kept walking until they came to a pair of swinging doors on their right with round windows in their centers. There were more trickles of water and shakes of thunder around them.

"This way," Raphael said. He held the doors open for the robot like it was a houseguest. They were inside a kitchen with rows of counters, cabinets, tables, and various other contraptions. It was pitch black, except for the beam of light piercing outwards from Raphael's arm. The room was cluttered with kitchen utensils, and pans. Despite the mess, Raphael scampered between all of it nimbly. He had every item memorized. TO knocked a metal tongs, which nearly fell off the counter, but Raphael jumped backwards and got it before it alerted the Phantom upstairs.

"Sorry," TO muttered.

Raphael took a deep breath and squinted.

"It's okay. You're doing good," he said. His voice trembled like he didn't believe what he was saying.

They eventually stopped at the end of the kitchen at a giant door, which was a walk-in freezer. It was silver, with a long handle in the middle. Raphael walked up to it and tapped it lightly with the nozzle of his shotgun.

"What was father's favorite drink?"

"Yahoo." A voice replied inside.

There was a clank, rush of air, and the door opened inwards.

A smaller boy jumped forward at TO.

"Oh my god, you got him to work. You did it. You really did Raph, I can't believe it," the boy said. He was shorter than Raphael, thinner, with spiked brown hair, pale skin, and a large coat hanging over his body. He wore a pair of goggles across his forehead. He had a big smile across his face, which was already a switch from Raphael.

"TO, this is Gabby," Raphael said, shutting the door behind the robot.

"Actually, my name is Gabriel," the boy said.

"Which title do you prefer for identification?" TO said.

"How about Gabriel?"

"Only mom and dad would call you that, and it was only when you'd be in trouble," Raphael said.

"So, whatever, I like it," Gabriel replied. "So yeah, robot, call me Gabriel."

"Hello, Gabriel."

"What do you say its name is? TO? That's kind of lame," Gabriel said.

"My authentic title is Tin One, Raphael shortened it to TO."

"Well, I like Tin One better, so we'll go with that, unless you get all pissy about it," Gabriel said.

"No, I don't care," Raphael said.

The room was dark and wide. A white lantern was nestled into the corner. Rows of shelves surrounded it. They were covered with canned food, machinery, batteries, clothes, and plastic containers. A pile of blankets was pushed up against the wall beneath the shelves. Above it, on the metal racks were a variety of pictures with faces in them.

"Not bad for a walk-in freezer, is it Bot?" Gabriel said, patting the machine's round chest. Raphael kicked the sheets into a pile and sat down on them with a grimace. He dug through a pile of books on his left and pulled out a Superman comic. The bold colors of its cover looked bright and luminous against the bleak rubble and shadow of the factory, which seemed to wrap the entire world in an abyssal hue.

"What happened to the world?" Tin One said. The words and their volume made Gabriel jump backwards.

"Remember, lower your volume. We're not the only ones here. Not by a mile," Raphael said.

"Ugh, Raph, are you even going to try and answer the question for him?" Gabriel said.

"What? Why? Why don't you explain it, Gabby?"

"You know you're going to complain about the way I tell him, so you might as well do it."

"It does not matter how the information is communicated, the data is essential for this unit's survival," Tin One said.

"Oh yeah, of course it is. I would want to know what was going on if I woke up to a fucking messed-up world." Gabriel said.

"Don't swear, Gabby." Raphael said.

"Well then tell him. You're just sitting there pretending to read a comic."

Raphael took a deep breath and rested his curly hair against the edge of the shelf. Tin One's vision wanted to focus on the pictures behind him, but it couldn't.

"We don't know what they were. We probably won't ever figure out what they are even. I'm not even sure we had the time to process it when they appeared. They were called the Silent Ones, because they showed up silently in our world." Raphael said. He stopped.

"How should I describe them, or the way they look or whatever?" Raphael said, looking up at the metal ceiling.

114

"Don't bother, there are skeletons just outside the factory. We can just show him sometime," Gabriel said.

"Yeah, that's true. So, the Silent Ones showed up and basically started eating everyone they could get their hands on. Millions of people died nearly instantly. The army attacked them, and there were battles in the streets and everywhere else. When the Silent Ones died, they released this strange gas into the sky and air. It blocked out the sun, changed the weather, and made it rain all the time. We were essentially screwed either way because either they attack and eat you, or we could kill them, and they'd poison the planet. Unsurprisingly, humanity took the destruction option and that's how the world got the way it is." Raphael said.

"Are the Silent Ones still active?" Tin One asked.

"Well, I think so, just not on the surface or anything. I remember mom and dad saying many of them had gone underground, which was lucky for us," Gabriel said.

"The high level of radiation in the environment is a product of their decomposition?"

"Yeah, yeah, absolutely. They let out some sort of pink gas. It didn't just cloud everything up either, it also made the bugs grow huge and our bodies change. A bunch of people mutated from it all." Raphael said.

"It was almost like they wanted us to kill them," Gabriel said.

There was a sudden slamming sound somewhere in the floors above them. Gabriel stepped away from the door and wandered over to the lantern tucked in the room's corner. He clicked the thin knob on its top and the white halo of energy faded like a frightened firefly.

"They're coming down here, don't speak," Raphael said.

Outside the room three forms entered the kitchen. They glided over and between every object without making a sound. The only time the Phantoms had to interact with their environment was when a door needed to be opened, or prey hunted.

"Let me take a look," Raphael said, silently stepping over to the door. Cut into the thick stainless steel of the freezer door was a small peephole to the kitchen. Raphael crushed his face up against it with a grimace. All he could see was bits of darkness illuminated by exit signs. Then he leered back and covered his mouth.

"They're right outside the door!" Raphael hissed to Gabriel, who immediately hid beneath the blankets.

"I guess you didn't actually distract them like you thought you would," Gabriel said.

115

"Shut up Gabby, they'll be gone in a few minutes, just let them have their fun and be quiet!" Raphael hissed. He crawled in tightly to his brother.

Tin One could take a hint. He stayed silent and still. After about ten minutes of pure silence, Raphael checked the door again. He sighed with relief and used the sleeve of his ripped-up sweatshirt to soak up the sweat on his forehead. Even though Tin One couldn't smell, watching the brothers act so nervous, the robot knew they stunk of panic.

"What happens if the Phantoms find you?" Tin One asked.

"They take you upstairs to the confinement area, which is basically just a room. They keep you there until the supervisor shows up and decides your fate," Raphael said.

"What does the supervisor do?"

"Ha, what supervisor? Almost everyone is dead. No one shows up, so you're stuck in a room and you starve to death. It happened to a bunch of our friends," Gabriel said.

"I'm sorry," Tin One replied.

"Way of the world now I'm afraid," Raphael said.

"It still sucks, Raph."

"I'm not saying it doesn't, Gabby."

"I can augment my sensors to detect the Phantoms before they arrive," Tin One said.

"That would be amazing. You're some sort of super Bot," Gabriel said.

"No, no, he has a Turing Matrix, so he learns as he goes," Raphael said.

He patted the giant robot on its round chest and smiled.

"He knows what we're worried about."

"Also of note, when I adjusted my microphones, I picked up footsteps on the stairwell," Tin One said.

"What? Like Human footsteps?" Gabriel said.

Tin One nodded.

"Is there any other kind?" It asked.

Raphael shook his head and closed his eyes. He wanted to be someplace else. Anywhere.

"Sadly, there is."

Phantom Security Drone: Series 72

Originally designed for standard building security in a manufacturing setting, Phantom Security Drones (PSD) were still effective after the Silent One's poisoned the earth's atmosphere. Running on kinetic batteries, all the units had to do to maintain their core energy was move. PSD's being programmed to patrol every fifteen minutes made it impossible for their batteries to ever dip below 50% charge.

In terms of quantity of eyewitness reports of what occurred after the apocalypse. PSDs were some of the most common independent robots still active on the earth's surface. Even as the Reclamation was taking place, more and more survey teams were finding renegade PSDs bent on arresting and imprisoning anyone who trespassed on their building. The PDS's elusiveness is one reason for this prominent level of survival. Able to outrun and escape insects and mutants, the wasteland didn't take many PSD's lives.

It was the surviving humans who had to reckon with them the most.

The Letter

It took a few moments for the brothers to stomach the thought of someone walking around the factory that wasn't a Phantom, insect, or mutant.

"Are you sure Tin One?" Gabriel asked, carefully approaching the freezer door.

"I'm fairly certain it is human footsteps judging by the pattern, weight, and frequency," Tin One replied in a mechanical echo.

"Well, well, we need to go out there and help them?" Gabriel said, turning back at his brother.

"Take it easy, Gabby. We don't know if they're mutants or not."

"How prevalent are mutations in this everyday environment?" Tin One said.

"Well, if something isn't mutated you wonder about it," Raphael said.

"Raph, you can't think every survivor that might stumble through this factory is a mutant. You got to have more hope than that."

"Quiet, Gabby."

"Geez, you're rude. Mom would say don't be rude to you right now."

"Mom's dead."

"My audio sensors have picked up breathing and coughing as well," Tin One said suddenly, sensing the awkwardness.

There was a distant yell. It cut through the dusty walls, floors, ceilings, and doors. It bounced off the shattered glass, piled plaster, and dangling electrical cords. It repeated like a skipping song or broken piano key.

"Help, help me," the scream said.

It traveled through the vents and walls in a desperate echo.

The two boys looked at the robot then back at another. Arguing over hope was easier than confronting a survivor on their very doorstep.

"We, we got to go," Gabriel said. Raphael bent down and picked up the torn backpack he'd been wearing when he activated Tin One.

"Your turn. I'm going to sit this one out," Raphael said.

"What? Really? Why? You don't care about saving anyone else," Gabriel said.

"Of course I do. I'm just not feeling well. I need to sit for a little bit. Take TO, or Tin One. He'll be more helpful than me.

Raphael bent down to show Gabriel the items zipped into the backpack. He avoided eye contact with his brother.

"Flare gun for insects. Shotgun for mutants. Slingshot to distract the Phantoms, or any other killer robot stalking about the factory." Raphael said.

"Of all the times to send me out by myself into this hellhole, don't you think you want me to be there to find another survivor?" Gabriel said, reaching for the backpack. Raphael held tightly to the straps as Gabriel pulled on it. The look in Raphael's eyes was a million miles away from the wasteland. A lone tear had gathered in a bloodshot corner of each eyelid. Gabriel was too annoyed to notice.

Raphael would not be alive much longer.

"You have to get used to doing things on your own a little bit. I can't always be there to help you," Raphael said, releasing the bag. He stepped backwards into the low light of the lantern, to hide how worried his face looked.

"Okay, well you need a haircut!" Gabriel said, pointing at his head. Raphael laughed.

"Yeah, whatever Gabby."

Gabriel brushed his hair back and went next to the door.

"Do you hear anything out there?" He said to Tin One.

"Just the bystander." The robot replied.

"Just go find them. The sooner you go, the sooner you get back here. I'm positive TO can protect you from the Phantoms at least for a few seconds," Raphael said. He grabbed Gabriel's shoulders and shifted him over to the handle of the door. In one quick shove, both Robot and boy were outside the freezer and standing in the darkness of the kitchen.

"Geez. I guess we'll get going," Gabriel said at the door.

"Hurry up." Raphael mumbled back.

Gabriel looked around the kitchen and touched the flashlight around his wrist. A beam of yellow broke the gloom. Gabriel started walking through the tables and counters in small steps. He had a different bounce to his walk than Raphael. It was healthy and energetic.

It was how a kid normally should be.

"Come on. Come on. Follow me, Tin One." Raphael said, walking to the swinging doors. He was through them and into the hallway without looking back. Further down the hallway from them, where the stairwell was from earlier, a large shape scuttled by. They stopped and Gabriel banged on the robot's chest with his hand.

"Got any lights on you to use?"

"I have 42 different lights available to use," Tin One said.

There was a hiss in the shadows. The sound seemed to crawl up the wall into the ceiling.

"Anyone will do!" Gabriel shouted, hiding behind Tin One's round body. A rectangular light bloomed on his chest in a clunk, throwing a glow onto the corridor. For a blinding instant, they watched the lower portion of a centipede drag itself upwards into the ceiling tiles. It was massive, as big as a German Shepherd, with length to spare.

"Is that? Is that an insect you've been referring to?" Tin One asked. It was the first time it had repeated a word in disbelief.

"Yeah, and that isn't even one of the big ones. There is one hanging out by the sewers we call Captain, because its head is so massive it looks like he's wearing an army helmet."

"This happened when the Silent Ones were eliminated?"

"Yeah, they were deadly themselves, but once they died, they made things even worse, which almost doesn't seem possible."

Gabriel started to gingerly walk down the hall.

"Keep that light on and that thing will stay away. Bugs might be bigger and scarier, but they still hate the light."

"Are you worried that the Phantoms might've already gotten the survivor?" Tin One said. He was following Gabriel towards the door.

"No. No. I mean I don't think so. We would've heard their screams. The Phantoms are exactly gentle when they grab you, you know."

Even basic walking was difficult due to the sheer volume of wreckage hanging on every surface. It was constantly above, below, around, behind, and in front of them. Tin One was programmed to grab and bring it to the proper reciprocals, but if that was going to be its task, it would take his lifetime to fulfill it in this wasteland. In a few seconds, the door was open to the stairwell. Gabriel grated his teeth when it moaned.

"Hurry, they might've heard that," he said, ushering Tin One up the stairs after him.

They hobbled up one flight and passed through a shattered doorway. There were dozens of deep scratches along the metal frame. Tin One noticed them and stopped.

"Don't ask," Gabriel said, grabbing the robot by the hand.

They were in some sort of lobby. In front of them was a large open room with a pair of square fountains sitting in the middle of the floor. They used to have water bubbling over them when the factory was working, but now they were poisonous cesspools. Beyond them were a set of elegant glass stairs up to the next floor.

"You can turn that light off, in the open we don't want to be spotted." Gabriel said. He wiggled the shotgun out from the backpack and snuck across the ground. Tin One ambled over and crouched down beside him. Gabriel was shaking. The air was cold, damp, and if Tin One could smell, rank with unending decay.

"Can, can you still hear them?"

Tin One increased the output to its microphones. Inside his half-globe head, it looked like a verdant radar line had just been thrown throughout the room. A few beeps from upstairs talked back, along with some below them.

"The human being is up the stairs and towards the showroom. The Phantoms are two floors beneath us investigating the sound of the insect."

"Okay, let's go," Gabriel said, shambling up the stairs. He stopped. "Common, let's go?"

"These will not support me. I will use my arms to grapple up."

Tin One aimed both arms at the railing attached to the stairs twenty feet above him. There was a friendly beep, a hiss, and a sudden pop of blue light around the machine's round arms of brown metal. His massive hands flew upwards in flash and grabbed onto the railing. They were still attached to his body in long, blue strings of plastic energy. In one quick snap, they coiled up, launching the robot upwards and over the barrier in one quick movement. His body slightly thudded the floor as he landed, but it didn't sound any louder than the random thunder from the storms outside.

"Well, that was pretty awesome." Gabriel said, grinning ear to ear.

A red light flashed outside the building through a broken bay window just above the door to the lobby. The Phantoms patrolled the grounds around the factory. Gabriel didn't mind that they did, there were plenty of nightmares trying to get inside their home on a daily basis. They were high up enough to almost look down on the mechanical shadows as they drifted by the empty parking lot outside.

"We don't have long. Can you pinpoint the sound?" Gabriel said. He played with the shotgun in his hand. He was making sure it was still there.

"My microphone indicates it is down this hall in the showroom," Tin One said. He pointed further down the corridor they were standing outside. There was a red carpet on the floor. When the factory still worked this area was considered the hall of fame. Along the wall were dozens of pictures of scientists, corporate professionals, and company executives.

Gabriel had no idea who any of them were, but he was certain most of them were dead.

"Tin One, are you a boy or a girl?" Gabriel asked as they snuck beneath the shattered pictures of bygone men.

"I have no assigned gender. I'm neither male nor female."

"Well, I think you should be a girl. I've got a brother, now I want a sister. Is that okay with you?" Gabriel said.

"It does not matter. I can fulfill either role; it is merely how you perceive me, that is all. Why would I fulfill the female sex?"

Gabriel stopped walking and looked down at the floor like he'd dropped something.

"You're nice to me like my mom was and all. I guess that just reminds me of her."

Tin One noticed Gabriel's chest tremble.

"It does not matter to me. Female it is."

The entrance to the showroom was through a pair of double doors. Both had been ripped off their hinges. Next to their gaping holes was a collection of claw marks and dents. Gabriel shook his head.

"That would've been a Silent One," he said, looking over his shoulder.

"I am confused by your statements earlier considering them, are they still in proximity to this location?" Tin One said.

"We're cryptic because we don't know. Raph swears they're all dead, I mean they were killable, and the army destroyed everything fighting with them, but we can't be, well, certain," Gabriel said.

They entered the showroom after a few minutes of listening and sprinted to a nearby wall inside the large room. The Phantoms were hopefully still occupied outside. Endless storms powered by the decaying corpses of monsters thudded against the foundation.

Even Tin One, who was not necessarily capable of emotion, was beginning to learn to be afraid of the current setting.

"Could my sensors pick up the Silent Ones you've described?"

"Technically, but a bunch of our technology was rendered useless against them. I'm not sure if you'd be able to or not, they were undetectable in a bunch of different ways," Gabriel said.

"I understand."

The ceiling was high and the walls far apart in the product showroom where they were. There were windows cut into the sloping roof in rectangles just above them. All of them were shattered, with trails of rain pouring inside and catching the lightning in flashing echoes. Throughout the gallery were dozens of stone pedestals standing like teeth. Atop them was every type of robot imaginable. Factory 9 was famous for its manufacturing capabilities when it came to artificial intelligence. Nursing Droids, Delivery Drones, Servant Androids, and War Machines were all represented atop these square altars to technological advancement. Sadly, many of these display models were destroyed or cannibalized. Survivors had used them to combat the Silent Ones. The only robot that wasn't destroyed in the showroom was a model of Tin One, which was missing its head.

"Raphael used that part to get you running. It was easier to switch parts into the display version. Much easier. Raphael's pretty good at all that technical stuff. Before the apocalypse, he used to sit in his room and watch videos about repairing stuff. Mom and Dad used to yell at him all the time to get outside and play like I was, but he never did. Guess it came in handy," Gabriel said. He was again staring at the floor when he spoke.

He was in another world, one of memory and love.

"Is that life sign still ahead?" He said, looking up at the robot.

"Affirmative, just at the end of the room."

"Let's go!" Gabriel said, dashing into the gloom.

The robot lumbered after him, trying not to disturb the strings of rubble scarring the room. The child was fleet of foot, but it took the entire machine's concentration to not bump their cluttered environment.

The shadows of the past robotic models loomed over the two as they snuck from pedestal to pedestal. A few times Tin One bumped against the structures. They had never been fastened to the ground, causing them to shake back and forth. Each time Gabriel hissed back at the robot. Gabriel had also asked him to turn the glare off his lights when they started moving, so not to be noticed.

"They should be directly in front of us," Tin One said.

Gabriel pulled the shotgun out from the pack and braced the butt into his shoulder. He was glad Raphael had taught him to shoot, even if he was impatient about it and yelled at him every time he missed. Shells were more valuable than food in this new, radioactive hell.

As they approached, the robot lunged forward, placing itself between the boy and the shapes. The Phantoms were there on the other side of the room. In the light you could see their tattered clothes, long limbs, and glowing lights. They had surrounded a woman on the floor. Only her feet were visible, followed by two long streaks of blood. The robots were standing like buzzards. Then, suddenly, there was a hiss of steam, then a sound of wet clothes and flesh being pulled. The phantoms had vanished with the person in tow through a pair of doors on the opposite side of the showroom. They moved so quickly Gabriel's eyes couldn't even interpret their movements.

The doors flapped closed.

Gabriel rushed forward to make sure the Phantoms were gone. He stared down at the stains and shook his head.

"Well, that's that. If that person was even alive, they're captured now and there's really no saving them. I guess we'll head back downstairs before they return. Plus, that blood might attract some insects."

"Wait, there is something on the ground," Tin One said, walking over to the red smears of faded life.

The robot leaned over and grabbed a small piece of paper off the ground.

"What's that?" Gabriel said, leering over it in the light.

124

Note: To Someone Out There

I'm only writing this down in case something happens to me. No, that's a lie. Something WILL happen to me. It is just a matter of time. So is my fate to wander the wasteland. In the basement of the Holiday Inn Parking Ramp, beyond the stairwells and last level, there is a storage room that was rented out by Hydroponics 2020 LLC. Inside the door there is a safe that contains hundreds of seeds for food and plants.

They were engineered to be radioactive resistant before civilization completely fell apart from the Silent Ones. They will work in this new world. Whoever gets this note, you need to go there. You need to find them. It is off Highway 35W and Washington Ave. It is the only parking ramp around. Next to it was Hydroponics 2020's headquarters.

You can find all the growing supplies you need there.

I don't know if we'll ever recover from what the Silent Ones did unless you do this. Please. My family is gone. I was out by myself trying to find help to retrieve the seeds. I can't do it alone.

-Rachel Vasquez, April 3rd, 2071.

Work

Ant and Fig knew they'd seen everything at least once before,
even if it was always nailed, sealed, and hammered into a wooden crate.
The two men had been employed at the piers together for six years. They
knew a highway of treasure had passed beneath their fingertips and gloves
as they lifted, twisted, pulled, pried, and wrenched boxes off the various
boats. The two men lived in Nibeah; a large merchant town nestled against
a green shore of velvet hills. All goods, items, relics, trinkets, ornaments,
antiques, or objects being sent to the country first passed through this
idyllic seaside town where wind chimes constantly played on patio
windows. Both men were constantly busy. It was a good thing. Time
passed quicker.

They hated their jobs.

Ant and Fig looked like each other. They were pale, greasy, and
rough looking. Each wore a pair of overalls with rips in the knees. Each
wore a red bandana to soak up sweat and keep the sea salt out of their
eyes. Both smoked. If you watched them carefully, the claws of smoke
creeping out of their lips and nose were identical as well. The only
difference between the two of them was their size. Ant was shorter. Fig
was taller. People always asked if they were brothers.

Neither cared enough to correct them.

Ant and Fig had been in Nibeah their entire lives. It was an
elegant looking city with stone buildings and cobblestone streets.
Windmills with bellies of gears turned between shadows and sunlight.
Quiet bridges over canals and windows of stained glass echoed laughter
and singing in the streets. There was money in the town thanks to the
constant merchants running their wares across the water and sky. There
was also an airship dock, so the winds were noisy with the groaning
propellers of zeppelins and their whistles.

Ant and Fig were stuck working late on the northern docks. The
night shift was difficult to work. The water was one long sheet of ink in
the gloom, with just the boat and lights to serve as beacons for their eyes.
It was the end of fall, where the air was slowly getting turned over by a
frosty dial. The lines of wooden steps, planks, and pillars were iced in
random spots. If you slipped and fell into the water, the night sky would
make you think you're caught between two oblivions.

Ant and Fig worked in a small shack on the edge of the pier
poking out into the deep. It had been a quiet night. They were reading
newspapers and letting a few cigarettes wither at their lips. They didn't
talk. They knew the same things. They thought the same things. What was

126

the point in speaking? All that mattered was them hearing the foghorn of the lighthouse sound. They could find that siren's song in their sleep if they had to.

It was close to 3:00 am when they finally got a ship crawling into the harbor on the still, dark waves. The sounds of the city were quiet. There were no blacksmiths hammering, gears twisting, or street performers summoning laughs and whistles on the boardwalks. The air smelt of cinnamon and yeast as the bakers made their first bout of delicacies in the few orange squares illuminated against a backdrop of black windows. A horn blew further up the docks. Ant and Fig opened the door of the dock house and walked onto the narrow pier, which jutted like a knife into the lapping water. A barge with a flat face and long wheelhouse was approaching them. A solitary lantern dangled from a post on its bow. The rest of the ship was empty of any light or movement. The vessel looked abandoned.

"Is that a riverboat? What's it doing here?" Ant said.

"Your guess is as good as mine. It's an old one too, doesn't even have railings along the hull," Fig said. He pointed a large hand at the flat nose of the ship. It was no doubt a vessel for hauling sand or some piled material, but this ship was empty of any crumbled mountain. Ant turned and walked back to the dock house and lit a red lantern. It was a signal for the horse and wagon to make the trek down to them.

"Well, I hope they don't have a ton of cargo, I mean it must all be inside the hull," Ant said. Fig threw a pair of thick ropes onto the deck of the boat and jumped down. Something was rancid on the ship. The odor grew heavier the closer you got to the wheelhouse. Fig got a heavy whiff of it.

"You're going to wake them up this time. I did it last time. I don't like doing it," Ant said.

"Fine, let's just wait for the horses to get here," Fig said.

Eventually an older man with a long cloud for a beard walked towards them smoking a pipe beneath a black hat. His name was Rufus, and he was the stable master for the docks. He'd known Ant and Fig their entire lives.

"Horses won't come down here for some reason, something's got them spooked. They even tried to jump in the water," Rufus said.

"Well, that's bad, how are we going to get the goods off? We'll have to wait until morning," Ant said.

"Have you boys even talked to the captain yet? Maybe they don't even have anything and just need to park," Rufus said.

"It stinks. It stinks badly," Fig replied.

127

"Well, it wouldn't be the first time we've gotten stinky wares onto the docks. You boys better talk to someone onboard and get this straightened out," Rufus said.

It took a few minutes for Fig to work up the courage to knock on the round door of the flat building stretched across the empty deck. It was cold and hollow against his rough hand. A scratching sound echoed inside the cabin. It made Fig jump back a second and steady his hand on the round doorknob, which was grimy brown from salt and rust.

"Hello? Anybody in there? You just reached Nibeah. You're at the northern pier. Come on out so we can get you checked-in," Fig said. A wave jostled the boat upwards.

The ocean was trying to warn him.

"Hello? I'm going to come inside. I just work for the docks." Fig turned the handle. It took some strength. Dust had frozen the bulkhead in place. Fig pushed on the door with his shoulder. After a few seconds it popped open. Fig fell into the room, banging his knee on the floor.

"You, you guys better get down here. Get down here now!" Fig screamed, crawling backwards like a crab onto the bow. Ant sprinted down the deck and lifted his friend up by the armpits. The door stared back at them. The lantern was turned on its side and threw some light into the cabin. Ant slowly approached the door and used his foot to steady the wobbling light. Ant lifted it up above his head with a gasp. The entire cabin was etched in dried blood. Benches, tables, ropes, fishing gear, bunks, bulkheads, the floor, even the candles locked into their fixtures were covered in this crimson smear. It was as if a giant vein had run the length of the building, then been split in one wild slash.

"What, what happened? Where is everyone?" Ant said.

Then it moved.

There was a hiss like a cat, but with more muscle and mass. It wasn't until the form dashed between both men out the doorway that they could decipher any details. All they could see was some sort of fluid body with slimy skin. The shape's arms were exaggerated and dragging on the floor, which was ripped apart thanks to the bits of gray bone spiking out of its shimmering flesh. Its head was that of an octopus. It had silver tentacles for hair, along with two red eyes with pulsating flaps. Its mouth looked human. A cloak, a satchel with a pair of books, and some legs with shredded pants hung off its rubbery body.

Before either man could turn to look at each other in amazement, the creature jumped off the deck and onto the dock in a few snarling bounds. Rufus, who was standing in the center of its path, could barely turn before the monster's long arms slashed outwards splitting his torso from his legs like wire through clay. There was a wet plopping of tissue. His body thrashed around as his upper-half tried to attach to his lower-

128

half. His howling scream made the night shake until shock got the better of him and he went eternally silent.

"Get back!" A voice said. It came from above the deck on the wheelhouse roof. There was a man standing there in the moonlight. He was tall, thin, with unblemished skin and sandy brown hair cut into a bowl. He was wearing some sort of priest's outfit, with a white collar and dark raincoat with baggy sleeves and enormous hood. His entire outfit appeared to change colors in the rolling night. He didn't want to be seen completely. In his right hand was an enormous silver gun with a wide barrel and gears poking out of its chambers. It had a pearl handle, which curled into the stranger's sleeve.

He raised the weapon into the air and clicked the trigger. Light thrashed the darkness in bits of sparks and fire. A blue flare curled into the sky above the dock and burst above it like a dying star. The creature froze and snarled backwards. It was already halfway towards the shore.

"You stay put!" The man yelled.

He was off the roof and onto the line of wooden planks before Ant or Fig could speak. He moved as a piece of the night, like the creature did.

"Watch out! Stay back!" He yelled. He loaded a few golden bullets into his gun with his sleeve. There was another hiss. The fiend had turned back towards the man. It swung its shadowy tendril of an arm at him. At the end of it, the bones had formed into a crude hammer. The man spun his coat over his right shoulder and braced for the impact. The cloth suddenly hardened into a golden shield. The bone and magic collided, throwing metallic thunder into the air and tossing the sea into a one-second tempest.

Ant and Fig were both knocked off their feet.

"Come on! Come on!" The man yelled. He pulled his shield away from the living brick. The monster's coil snapped back. The air cackled to it. The man fired twice from his pistol. The monster jumped, sending both shots into empty air. It twirled violently and severed its own arm throwing the organic flail through the air. The man once again threw his coat up and smashed into the missile. The impact shattered the dock. Shrapnel cut the air. Some of the splinters hit Ant and Fig, who were frozen in awe.

It wasn't every day that monsters and gods threw fire at each other.

The creature dashed further from the man. The attack was to distract him and slow him down. The man hunched over and coughed up some blood. It looked unreal in the dark of the moon and torchlight. He shook his head and took to one knee. He leveled the gun at the shape. The monster was approaching the buildings at the end of the pier. A small crowd had gathered to watch the ruckus. The flare had woken them up.

129

"Goddammit!" The man said with a wheeze. He hit a red gear planted alongside the oblong chamber of his firearm. Fire cut the air in a perfect line. A beam of white light opened from the atoms around the barrel and engulfed the dock. It narrowed as it spread in a fine, sharp laser. It struck the abomination in the back of its head. The momentum from the blast tossed its body into the water and onto the dock in steaming chunks.

"Got it," the man said. He collapsed onto his stomach.

Ant and Fig didn't move. Fig was holding Ant by the shoulders. They were practically hugging one another. They were about to speak when the man wheezed and slowly stood up. He pulled the hood over his young face and stretched out beneath his coat. A few bones and joints cracked. He'd been hurt before.

"What do you guys do?" he asked in an older voice. It was bold and rough. It didn't match the softness of his youthful appearance.

"What, what?" Ant said.

"Did you not hear me? What do you guys do for a living?" He shook the gun free of the water that had sprayed during the fight.

"We, uh, work on the docks," Ant said.

"I realize that. But what do you do? What does your job entail?"

A few people screamed at the other end of the dock. The monster's rubbery parts were trying to reconnect. The man sighed. He would have to burn the leftovers.

"We move boxes. We unload them and load them. That's it," Fig said.

The man lifted his gun and looked down the square sight jutting out from the still steaming nozzle. He sighed and started walking towards the monster's sour and ambitious remains.

"That sounds nice," he said.

130

What was I thinking?

Erasmus: This character is key to the entire narrative of the Greenland Diaries, including the past, current, and future. Erasmus is obviously a Reanimated, but a very perfect and special one. The Unnamed clearly want him to live. He can also hear voices and communicate with them. Instead of having any sort of break in the story or pause within the narrative, I went full bore with the story to make it seem as overwhelming as it did to poor Erasmus. There have been subtle hints dropped from the Unnamed about what they're after with the drum and their very existence. As the main journal narrative continues towards an end, these motivations will become more apparent. Erasmus is the epiphany of this concept. He will return in the Greenland Diaries, and the sequel series "The Jade," which is way down the road, but a certainty. This part of the story will focus completely on the forest that crops after the destruction of the drum. I can't wait to get there and for you all to experience it.

Key Largo: First off, I absolutely adore Key Largo. It has a special place in my heart for many reasons. I really wanted to explore the tropical setting in this apocalypse and Key Largo had the most memories for me to pull from. Often, I take pieces of my nonfiction life and inject them into my fiction, especially when it comes to producing real and emotionally relatable sensory details. The tropics sort of called me because I have written A LOT about the Twin Cities with this series. Needed a slight change in scenery. Plus, this gave me the opportunity to focus on the Water Unnamed, and even draft a story from her point-of-view. You know I love to explore that perspective. One last point about these bits of narrative. One thing I've pointed out with the Greenland Diaries is that those who challenge the monsters tend to die, and the ones who hide survive. With Key Largo, I wanted to demonstrate this a little bit more clearly.

The Three Clawed Man: Speaking of writing from a monster's perspective, I'm not sure if it gets more monstrous than my beloved Three-Clawed Man. His voice is violent, nostalgic, and hideously logical. I wanted to really get into his character and motivations right away with his voice. He's also a perfect opportunity for an exposition dump for my BTI universe. His introduction is pivotal to the continuation of the story. Not only is he a villain, but he's also a bit of a hero. A nice gray line in the morality chart. I can only write characters with this complexity. I wouldn't have any interest in them if they were all good or bad. How bland. This character's strength is on par or surpasses the Guardian. I can't wait to unleash it. He's very worth the wait. I also wanted to include the berserker from Beware the Ills. I wanted that dialogue and interaction right away with this character, to establish time and resonance with the first book.

Leave the Name: The title story of this collection. It is exactly what you wanted. The new Guardian, fresh off the ritual, entered the woods for the first time. I knew I wanted to have them be female. I wanted that perspective, and is turns out, there have been many Guardians before, many of whom were female. The sword is obviously haunted and part of a greater conspiracy. It changes everyone in a separate way, much like violence itself on a metaphorical level. Once you commit an act of harm to someone or something, you change into others who have done similar actions, while also staying yourself. The sword takes this concept to a far sharper degree. This new Guardian POV also gave me the opportunity to give even more exposition to the Diamond Town and its inhabitants. The ceremony of her signing her name on a rock and leaving it in a pool, ties to a direct scene from Beware the Ills where the previous Guardian is swimming but can't remember why they are there. Turns out his name was written on a rock just a few feet below the water. He can't tell you his name because he cannot remember it. He gave it up to the island, just like her.

The Shingles: I really wanted to revisit this location from Beware the Ills. In that book, the Guardian perches on them, but doesn't really use them as a fortress or setting of note when it comes to the plot. In this story, the Three Clawed Man sneaks through,

132

introducing a little bit of mayhem. We're also given some dialogue between an Ill and this antagonist. That was a really a lot of fun to write. I also got to describe the Shingles and the Diamond Town from a unique perspective, so the audience could see it a bit more vividly. These three stories I included in this collection are the beginning of the sequel to Beware the Ills, which I thought would never have a counterpart, but here we are a decade or more later from its original publication, with one at least half done. So much more to come of the Cursed Island.

A Rose for Walter: My good ole' rip-off of Faulkner's classic tale that I wrote for the podcast Hidden Oaks. Here I got to sort of use nonfiction elements from my life when my father had the motivation to be a bit more controlling and micromanaging towards me. Here we have an undead element, which was fun to write. I can't imagine what it would be like living with a corpse that comes back to life. I tried to make it as atmospheric and claustrophobic as possible. Walter reanimates thanks to the presence of She, a totally unique monster imprisoned in a nearby park called Hidden Oaks. Her very presence causes fluctuations of the supernatural throughout the neighborhood.

Star Ocean Foods: This one was a lot of fun to write because I have a huge affinity for Asian grocery stores. There were also a few next to me where I grew up next to Hidden Oaks that I never explored as a kid, but certainly wished I had. This story is like a Rose for Walter, where something supernatural and strange is happening both intentionally and randomly to someone living near our lovely monster. This story follows the character's own natural trajectory towards escapism. Will wants to flee his mundane suburban life through the diversity and uniqueness of this store, which thanks to this supernatural entity, obliges a little too ardently.

The Butterfly: I had been dreaming and thinking about a haunted butterfly for years. Also, the scene where the toys float up in the water around the playground was something I had been toying with (ha ha) since I was in college writing my senior project. Playgrounds have always had a creepy undertone in terms of symbolism. They sort of mark a loss of innocence when you revisit them in your memories. It isn't just nostalgia that you feel but longing for a moment where life seemed so much grander and innocent.

Factory 9: For this one, I thought I'd lump all the pieces together. Factory 9 was conceived and partially executed before the Greenland Diaries. Unfortunately, it did not have the same energy with me creatively as that apocalyptic series did, and I sort of abandoned it partway through. Factory 9 is inspired by the famous JRPG Chrono Trigger, specifically its future world you venture through at various points in the game. Factories with uncontrollable robotics were a common interaction in this devastated post-Lavos atmosphere. That dynamic fascinated me as a storyteller. Would these machines have any purpose without us around? Would they just continue with their original programming. The Phantoms were a perfect example of this concept. Can you imagine a security system kidnapping you and leaving you in a room for someone to never show up? With Factory 9 I also wanted to practice writing child characters. I based a lot of their dynamics and personalities on my former stepsons. The dialogue. The flow of words between characters. It was all carefully crafted. Strangely, for someone who writes very dark stories (I mean the Unnamed cut people apart and resurrect them as sewn together monsters), Factory 9 was too dark for me to continue writing. I will revisit it someday. Their story deserves to be told.

Work: A special, bonus short story for this collection. This is a story I've been kicking around for many years. It even appeared in one of my fiction courses about twenty years ago at the U of M when I was taking creative writing classes. Darn thing kept bullying me around, so I took another shot at it. This story I really wanted to have a couple of guys who sort of loath their mundane jobs and get exposed to a seemingly much worse occupation. In this case, a random hunter with a badass gun hunts a squid person across the sea. Yet another sentence I can't believe I just wrote. Moving those boxes isn't so bad when you're caught in a bloody battle with some sort of octopus demon.

Well, everyone, thank you again for supporting my work through this journey. There is so much more to come. The sequel to Beware the Ills, two more books in the Greenland Diaries, and new projects and series. I'm blessed and fortunate to have been doing this for the last ten years. Thank you everyone. It is a privilege.

To learn more about Patrick W. Marsh please visit his website www.patrickwmarsh.com.

Thank you.

Made in the USA
Monee, IL
01 October 2025